THE SUMMER BEFORE

THE SUMMER BEFORE

ANN M. MARTIN

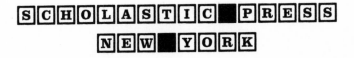

SCHOLASTIC PRESS NEW YORK

Library of Congress Cataloging-in-Publication Data Available

ISBN 978-0-545-16093-3

10 9 8 7 6 5 4 3 2   10 11 12 13 14

Printed in the U.S.A.   23
First edition, April 2010

The text type was set in Palatino.
Book design by Steve Scott

For Jean Feiwel, David Levithan,
Brenda Bowen, and Bethany Buck—
from the beginning to the end
and back to the beginning

Special thanks
to my nephew Henry
for introducing me to Tail Trail
and the naked mole rat, and
to Haedyn and Holden Riley
for inventing the game
of Sticky

1   KRISTY

The Baby-sitters Club. I'm proud to say it was totally my idea, even though the four of us worked it out together. "Us" is Mary Anne Spier, Claudia Kishi, Stacey McGill, and me—Kristy Thomas. But that was at the beginning of seventh grade, after the summer in which my friendship with Claudia nearly fell apart, Mary Anne began to find out who she was, Claudia experienced her first love, and an unhappy girl left New York City and moved to our town. It was quite a summer.

When Mary Anne and Claudia and Stacey and I talked about it later (when we were older), we discovered that during those long hot months we had all, separately, felt that we didn't quite belong where we were. Not one of us. Up until that summer we hadn't paid much attention to such things. But now Mary Anne felt that she was suddenly teetering between childhood and teenagehood, or whatever you call it, and that she didn't fit into either world. Claudia felt that she was drifting away from Mary Anne and me, drifting toward

1

her own teenagehood alone—while Mary Anne and I lingered on the shore. Stacey had survived a horrible year and had been shunned by her classmates and friends, and now her parents had decided to move the family here to Stoneybrook, Connecticut, where she knew absolutely no one. And I, Kristin Amanda Thomas, felt like a stranger in my family. I would look around at my mom and my brothers, who were oh-so-happy with Mom's new boyfriend, Watson, and I'd think, How can they leave Dad behind? Am I the only one who still wants him to be part of the family? And so I decided to give my father a second chance.

The summer started off like most of the other summers of my life. But by the end of it, everything was different. *We* were different. And the summer brought the four of us, Claudia, Stacey, Mary Anne, and me, together to form the Baby-sitters Club—something we would belong to, in one sense or another, for the rest of our lives.

*   *   *

When the bell rang at the end of the last day of sixth grade, I was ready. I had cleaned out my locker early that morning before school began—and I mean *really* cleaned it. With a tiny bottle of Fantastik and a bunch of paper towels that I had stuffed into my backpack before I left home. I had removed every last scrap of paper from the locker, every old eraser, every gum wrapper and paper clip and pencil stub, plus one gray sock, and thrown them away (including the sock, which smelled). Then I had scrubbed the locker down with the Fantastik. I wasn't taking any chances on being called at home in a day or two about the condition of my locker. I did not want to have to set foot in Stoneybrook Middle School again until September, when seventh grade would begin. So when that last bell rang, I ran from my language arts class (calling a hasty and not at all heartfelt good-bye over my shoulder to Mrs. Alpin, whom I loathed) directly to the front door of SMS, where I met Mary Anne, my best friend in the world. Mary Anne had also cleaned her locker thoroughly that morning, and the two of us had not one single school responsibility left.

We had to wait for Claudia, though. Claud had not thought quite as far ahead as we had, and she still had to deal with her locker and also have a chat with her math teacher, whose class she had not exactly flunked but hadn't quite passed, either. These were Claud's words, and while they didn't make sense to me, I didn't care. School was out!

"You know what my grandmother used to shout on the last day of school?" I said to Mary Anne as we waited, lolling against the door frame and watching kids stream past us, calling and hooting.

"No. What?" I could tell that Mary Anne was impatient for Claudia to show up.

"She used to shout, 'School's out! School's out! Teacher wore her bloomers out!'"

Mary Anne stared at me. "What does that mean?" she said finally.

"Well, how should I know? It just sounds funny."

Mary Anne twirled the end of one brown braid thoughtfully around her finger. "Maybe—" she started to say.

But I interrupted her. "There's Claudia."

Mary Anne turned around and we saw Claud coming toward us through the crowded corridor at a pace ordinarily reserved for snails and turtles. She was walking arm in arm with Dori Wallingford. Howie Johnson and Pete Black were flanking them.

"Dori," Mary Anne muttered.

"Boys," I muttered.

Claudia and Mary Anne and I used to sit together at lunch sometimes, but that had changed between our winter break and our spring break. Dori and several other girls who were more interested in clothes than in practically anything else had suddenly become more interesting to Claudia than Mary Anne and me or practically anyone else. Except boys.

Claudia waved cheerfully to her new friends.

4

"See you!" she called as Dori and Howie and Pete crossed the lawn to the line of waiting school buses. "Hi, you guys," she said to Mary Anne and me, and for an instant I felt like something hanging on the Reduced rack at Bellair's Department Store.

"Hey, Claud," said Mary Anne as we began our walk to Bradford Court, "what do you think 'Teacher wore her bloomers out' means?"

Claud shrugged and snapped her gum.

Mary Anne tried again. "So, what are you guys doing this afternoon?"

Now Claudia answered in an instant. "Nothing. Wonderful, glorious nothing. That is the beauty of no homework." She paused, then added thoughtfully, "Well, not really nothing. I think I'll paint."

"I'm baby-sitting for David Michael," I said. David Michael was my six-year-old brother. My big brothers (Charlie, who was sixteen, and Sam, who was fourteen) and I took turns watching him when school was out. While our mom had a great job at a company in Stamford, the salary wasn't enough to support four children *and* a nanny. Our parents were divorced and Dad, who had remarried and lived all the way across the country in California, sent money when he felt like it. The temporary jobs he got didn't pay much, so Mom always said, "You can't squeeze blood out of a stone." (When you think of it, you can't squeeze anything out of a stone, but I knew what she meant.)

We reached Bradford Court, where Claudia, Mary Anne, and I had grown up. It was weird to think that eleven years earlier we had all been babies on this street, Mary Anne and I next door to each other and Claudia across from us. Our parents were young then, my mom and dad still married, no David Michael yet, Mary Anne's mother still alive. Had our parents hung out together the way we did now? I'd have to ask my mom about that sometime.

I noted Louie's exuberant barking from inside my house and realized he must have been sitting against the front door.

"I'd better let Louie out," I said.

"I'm going to start painting!" Claudia cried before running across the street.

"And I'm—I'll see you later," said Mary Anne mysteriously.

"Wait. What are you going to—" I started to say, but Mary Anne was already halfway across her lawn. She waved to me over her shoulder.

"Huh," I said, and unlocked the front door.

Louie, our aging collie, practically bowled me over in his rush to get outside. "Hey," I said to him, "here come Charlie and David Michael." It was Charlie's turn to pick up David Michael from afternoon kindergarten.

Louie greeted them energetically as they hurried, hand in hand, along our front walk, David Michael gleefully waving his free hand to show me that it was empty of pencils and workbooks.

"He's all yours," exclaimed Charlie, making a show of removing David Michael's hand from his and placing it in mine.

"Where are you going?" I asked him.

"Over to Hank's. Baseball. Back by dinnertime," he said in a rush as he tossed his backpack through the door. Then he loped down Bradford and around a corner.

"Hey! What about me?" asked David Michael, looking forlornly after Charlie.

"It's okay," I said. "We'll have fun this afternoon."

I let David Michael and Louie inside the house and we walked through the cool, quiet rooms to the kitchen. "Just think," I added as I removed two apples and some cheese sticks from the refrigerator, "this is the last after-school snack you'll have to eat until September. For the next ten weeks," (I had counted, many times) "they'll just be regular snacks."

David Michael smiled at that and his grin broadened as he said, "I'll bet we get hoagies for dinner tonight!"

"Hoagies. Why?" I asked suspiciously. I liked hoagies, but . . .

"Because Mom's going out with Watson."

"What? Again?" My mother had just gone out with her so-called boyfriend five days ago. It seemed to me that their dates were taking place more and more often. In May, when she had first met him, they'd gone out exactly twice. Now it wasn't even the end of June and they'd already seen each other four more times. Four *more* times, for a total of six—that I knew about.

"Kristy," said David Michael, "pay attention. You're baby-sitting for me tonight. Remember? Mom's paying you? That's because of the date, duh."

"Oh. Yeah." I guess I just hadn't wanted to think too deeply about Watson.

While we ate our snack, David Michael told me a long story about a boy in his class who, at snack time that day, had first said he felt like he was going to barf, then had said he felt okay, then had gagged, although nothing further had happened for five minutes, and finally had barfed in a rather spectacular manner all across the snack table.

"But none of it got on me," concluded my brother with some pride. "Or on my snack."

"Well, thank goodness," I replied. Because I was eager to change the topic, I added, "Want to go to the playground this afternoon?"

"The *school* playground?" asked David Michael, horrified. "No!"

"The one in the park, then."

"Okay."

So we spent an enjoyable two hours swinging on the swings, climbing on a make-believe pirate ship, hanging from the monkey bars, and shooting down the corkscrew slide. We returned home just in time to see Mom emerge from her car, then reach into the backseat for a large bag with the words *Hoagie Heaven* scrawled across one side.

"Told you so," said David Michael, and my mood darkened immediately.

My dismal mood was shared by not one single other member of my family. All of my brothers were thrilled with the hoagies and later seemed happy enough when Watson appeared at our front door. (I noted that Watson didn't ring the bell, simply knocked twice, called "hello" through the screen door, and let himself in before anyone had answered him.)

"All right," said Mom as she stood smiling in the hallway with her *date*, "Kristy's in charge of David Michael tonight. Sam and Charlie, you're on your own. I'll be home by ten. Kristy, you know where the emergency numbers are. Watson and I will be at Chez Maurice."

Chez Maurice. The fancy French restaurant.

"Ooh-la-la," I muttered.

Mom heard this but ignored me. "Bedtime at nine for David Michael. Summer hours."

"Wahoo!" cried David Michael, whose school bedtime was considerably earlier.

By nine-fifteen, David Michael was asleep and Sam and Charlie were at a friend's. For a few moments, I wandered through our quiet house, glad for Louie's company, wondering what to do next. And then . . . I surprised myself.

Isn't it funny how every now and then you think you're just about to, say, turn on the TV or open a book, and instead you find yourself doing something else altogether, something you hadn't even been thinking about? That was what happened then, in those silent moments. Without knowing that I was going to do it, I found a pen and a pad of paper, sat down at our kitchen table, and began a letter to my father.

It had been nearly five months since I had written to him and even longer since I'd heard from him. So why did I suddenly feel the need to contact him? I wasn't sure, but I felt it was time to fill him in on my life since February. There were so many things he didn't know, unless Mom was in touch with him, and she probably was, but still. I hadn't told Dad about my grades this semester (they were good), or that I had started baby-sitting for some of the kids in our neighborhood, or that I had missed an entire week of school because of strep throat or that Mary Anne and I were frequently shocked by the outfits Claudia

10

put together these days, or that Mom and Mr. Watson Brewer had begun a dating marathon.

I wondered if I should mention Watson, or whether Mom had mentioned him herself. Then I wondered what, exactly, it was that I hoped to accomplish by being in touch with my father again. Well, of course, part of it was simply that he was my father and I wanted to stay connected to him. That was obvious. But there was something else. One little molecule of me hoped he could be part of our family again, that things could be the way they used to be. I knew this was foolish. He and Mom had been divorced for years, Dad was remarried and lived three thousand miles away, and Mom was interested in other men, or at least in Watson. But I didn't care. I wanted Mom and Dad and my brothers and me all living in the same house again.

Also, my birthday was coming up in August and I was curious to see whether Dad would do anything about it. He had come through with a card the year before, but we'd been in touch more often then. I considered including a gentle reminder in my letter ("Can you believe that your daughter is almost twelve years old?"), but then I decided that anything he might send me would mean a whole lot more if he remembered my birthday on his own. So finally I wound up the letter with a cheery "Have a great summer!"

as if I were signing his yearbook. I sealed the envelope, stamped it, and addressed it using the return address from the note Dad had sent me over the winter. I wasn't certain it was up-to-date, since Dad moved around a lot, but I crossed my fingers and hoped for the best.

I was just sneaking the letter underneath a stack of to-be-mailed envelopes waiting on a table in the front hallway when the phone rang. I made a dash to answer it before it woke David Michael.

"Hello, Thomas residence," I said.

"Kristy? This is Mrs. Pike."

My heart jumped. Mrs. Pike was mother to the eight Pike kids and sometimes asked me to baby-sit for the younger ones. It would be nice to earn a little money, plus I was hoping to work on my sitting skills over the summer.

"Mr. Pike and I have a meeting to go to next Thursday evening," Mrs. Pike continued, "and I was wondering if you could baby-sit. All eight kids will be at home, though, so I think we'll need two sitters. I just spoke to Claudia and she isn't available. Can you do it? And do you know of anyone else who could come with you?"

"I'm available," I said, pleased, "but can I call you back tomorrow about the other sitter? I'm sure I can find somebody."

As soon as I finished the call I began to punch in numbers on the phone again. Then, abruptly, I hit the OFF button. I'd been about to call Mary Anne, but two things had stopped me. One was the time. Mary Anne's strict father didn't let her talk on the phone after dinner on school nights. But this was summer vacation. Still . . . was it too late? I decided it wasn't but then considered my other concern: Although Claudia and I had started sitting earlier in the year, and I'd had plenty of experience watching David Michael, this would be Mary Anne's very first job.

After staring at the phone for several more moments, as if the buttons could help me make a decision, I punched in the Spiers' number after all. Mr. Spier answered the phone, but he didn't sound upset and Mary Anne picked up the extension right away.

"Good news!" I said to her brightly. "Mrs. Pike called and she needs two baby-sitters for next Thursday evening. Want to come with me?"

"What? To *baby*-sit?" Mary Anne's voice had risen to an alarming squeak.

"Yeah. It'll be fun."

"But I've never sat before. I don't know if Dad will let me."

"Could you talk to him about it? After all, Claudia and I baby-sit. And we're all the same age."

"I really *want* to start sitting," said Mary Anne. "But . . . you know Dad."

Mr. Spier was the strictest parent I'd ever met, probably because he'd had to raise Mary Anne on his own after her mother had died. Still . . .

"Your father has to let you grow up sometime," I pointed out.

"It would be so much fun to baby-sit," said Mary Anne rapturously. "I love little kids."

"You're really good with David Michael," I said encouragingly.

"Oh, but I'd be so nervous! What if something went wrong? What if we had to call the police?"

"The po*lice*? I have never once had to call the police while I was baby-sitting."

"Aren't you afraid to be in charge?"

"No. I love being in charge." Now I was wondering if calling Mary Anne had been a good idea after all.

"Let me talk to my father," she said. "I'll call you tomorrow."

"Okay," I replied.

I hung up the phone, wandered to the kitchen, and looked out the window. And that was when I saw the first shooting star of the summer. I should have felt elated. Instead, I sensed trouble.

2 MARY ANNE

My room was so pink that sometimes I would lie in bed and feel as though I were drowning in a rose-colored river. My rug was pink, the frames around the pictures were pink, the rosebuds on the wallpaper were pink, the curtain fabric was pink floral, and the curtains themselves were tied back with pink ribbons. Sadly, pink was my least favorite color. (I liked yellow and navy blue.) But my father had decorated the room for me when I was two, and that was what he'd thought a little girl would like.

On the morning of the first full day of summer vacation, I lay in my bed, adrift in that river of pink, and thought about Kristy's offer the night before. Was I ready to be a baby-sitter? Well, I *wanted* to baby-sit. But I wanted to do a lot of other things, too, such as live by myself in New York, the most romantic city in the world, but of course I wasn't ready to do that, and I wasn't certain I was ready to baby-sit, either.

I tried to imagine the conversation in which I would ask my father if I could try baby-sitting. "Dad," I would say, "Kristy asked me something last night."

My father would look at me and see his little girl with her braids (which I wore at his insistence, not because I thought they were fashionable), sitting across from him in one of the outfits he had chosen for her, and say, "Yes?" (My father never, ever said "yeah.") "What did she ask you?"

"She asked me if I could baby-sit with her at the Pikes' house."

At this point, my imagination ground to a halt. What I hoped my father would then say was, "How wonderful. What a very grown-up offer. I'm sure the job will go just fine." But what I was pretty sure he would actually say was, "Mary Anne, that's out of the question. You're not old enough to baby-sit." Which was a lame argument for a lawyer to make, considering that Kristy and I were the same age.

I sighed, rolled over, and looked at the framed pictures of *Alice in Wonderland* characters and Humpty Dumpty that adorned my walls. What I wished for on my walls instead — wished for mightily — were a poster of New York City, a poster of Paris at night, and, well, maybe a poster of a kitten.

16

I peered at my clock. Dad had probably already left for work. I yawned and made my way downstairs to the kitchen. As I had suspected, Dad was gone. A note from him was on the table, propped against a glass. It read:

Good morning, sleepyhead! Happy first day of summer vacation! Please do the following: 1. Check in with me at the office before 9:30 and any time you leave the house. 2. Eat breakfast, and be sure it includes fruit and milk. 3. Eat a proper lunch. 4. Run the washing machine. 5. Take the ground beef out of the freezer so we can have hamburgers for supper.
Love, Dad
P.S. Have fun.

I thought the P.S. looked rather hastily written, as if the true meaning of summer vacation had just occurred to Dad. Then I picked up the phone to let him know I was awake and alive. After that, I checked the locks on all our doors to make certain no one could sneak up on me while I was in the bathroom or not paying attention. Then I ate a fruit-and-milk-inclusive breakfast, and finally I got around to my current favorite activity: searching through my mother's past.

My father didn't know I was doing this. He didn't have a clue that I'd been in our attic and found the box belonging to my mother. As far as Dad was concerned, the attic was the perfect hiding place for things he didn't want me to see, because I was afraid of its dark corners and creepy, secretive noises. But one day in April when Dad had been at work and I'd been at home with a cold, I had braved the attic in search of a quilt and had come across a cardboard carton labeled ALMA, which was my mother's name. I had reached for it very cautiously, afraid it might harbor mice or spiders, and had brought it all the way back to my bedroom before I dared to open it. When I did, I found it, thankfully, to be both mouse- and spider-free and, more important, to be packed—tightly—with items that had belonged to my mother.

There were things from her childhood and things from her adolescence and things from her college years and even things from when she was pregnant with me. Which was fascinating, since apart from the fact that my father blessed my mother during grace before dinner every evening, we rarely mentioned her. The box held clues to my mother, and I was eager to learn as much as I could. But I felt I had to do so without Dad knowing about it. In fact, I had mentioned the box only to Kristy and had shown it to no one.

My favorite things in the box were my mother's dolls. There were four of them, and they were medium-size—bigger than Barbies, smaller than American Girls. They weren't fancy, they weren't antiques, and they weren't valuable, except to me. To me, they were four keys to Alma Baker Spier.

I lined up the dolls on my bed and undressed them, thinking that I should make each one a new outfit. I wondered what kind of clothes my mother might have made for them when she was little. Before I had any ideas, I was interrupted by the doorbell. I ran down the stairs, dressed in capri pants, a blouse, and sandals (all chosen for me by Dad, of course), and peered through the front window. I was forever afraid I'd find a stranger at the door, but the person on the stoop was Kristy.

"Hi!" I greeted her. Kristy looked considerably more casual than I did, but then she was allowed to choose her own clothes, and sometimes she even got to wear hand-me-downs from Sam and Charlie, which was very cool. She said nothing about my blouse or floral pants, though, just barged inside and said, "Did you ask your father yet?"

"About baby-sitting? No. He left for work before I got up. I'm going to talk to him at dinner tonight."

"Well . . . all right. I told Mrs. Pike I'd call her today. So make *sure* you talk to your dad at dinner."

"I will. I promise."

"So what are you doing?"

"Come upstairs and see," I replied.

There were the four nude dolls, their clothes in a pile on the pillow.

"You're playing dolls?" said Kristy, wrinkling her nose.

"No. Fashion designer. I'm going to make new outfits for them."

Kristy immediately looked bored. "Let's go outside," she said.

"Don't you want to know where the dolls came from?"

"What do you mean?"

"Well, they don't look familiar to you, do they?"

"I don't know," said Kristy in a way that suggested that all dolls looked pretty much the same to her. "I guess not."

"They were my mother's," I informed her. "They were in the box."

"Oh!" The dolls might not have held any interest for Kristy, but my mother did. Kristy sat on the edge of the bed and pulled one of the dolls toward her. "Your mother must really have liked these if she kept them until she was a grown-up and married and everything."

"I think she was saving them for me."

"She probably always hoped she would have a girl. She must have been really happy when you were born."

I smiled. "So come on. Let's get sewing. All their clothes are dingy from being in that box for so long."

"Let's get *sew*ing?!" exclaimed Kristy. She stopped just short of saying, "Are you crazy?"

"Please?" I begged.

"I don't know how to sew."

"I'll teach you."

"Can I look through the box instead? While you sew?"

I sat down on the bed and glanced at the box, which was between Kristy and me. I pulled it into my lap. "I—no. I mean, the box is sort of private."

Kristy blushed. "Sorry." Then she said, "I have an idea. What if we take the dolls over to Claudia's? Maybe she could give you some suggestions for their new clothes."

I hesitated. "Well, maybe." I hadn't told Claudia about the box or the dolls. And nobody knew exactly how much time I spent looking through it. But none of that mattered. Claud was awfully creative and certainly more sophisticated than Kristy and I. Even if I didn't always like her outfits, I had to admit that they were fashionable.

I looked at the dolls, at their old clothes, at my

pink-and-white ensemble, at Kristy in her blue jean cutoffs and SHS VARSITY SOCCER T-shirt, which apparently had once belonged to Charlie, and suddenly I said, "Okay. Let's go! But I have to call Dad first."

"When is he going to let go of that rule, I wonder," said Kristy. "You'd think his rules would change as you grow up."

I sighed. "He still sees me as three years old. . . . Well, maybe six."

"Either way, it's a problem," said Kristy.

I gathered up the dolls, then phoned Dad at his office and told him Kristy and I were going across the street. We had just stepped onto the front stoop, my arms laden with the dolls, when we heard a car door slam and saw Claudia about to climb into her family's station wagon, her grandmother Mimi at the wheel.

"Wow, look at Claudia," said Kristy breathily.

Claudia was wearing willowy black pants, cinched at the waist with a drawstring, and a boldly patterned summer shirt with ties that she was adjusting around her midriff. Her midriff would have been bare, but Claud had slithered into a lacy black tank top before she'd put on the shirt. On her feet were delicate silvery sandals, and her hair, which was loooooong and thick, was held away from her face with two silver combs.

22

"Wow," I echoed. "I don't think the dolls should dress like that."

Claudia saw us as she slid into the front seat and waved.

"Where are you going?" Kristy called to her.

"Art class!" Claud called back. "See you later."

Kristy and I turned around. "Now I have to call my dad *again* and tell him I'm home after all," I said, and Kristy made a sympathetic face.

★   ★   ★

Late that afternoon, the laundry done and supper underway, I decided to set the table in the dining room instead of the one in the kitchen. It couldn't hurt, I thought, to butter up Dad with a fancy dinner before I broached the subject of baby-sitting. I placed flowers on the table and found our good napkins and place mats.

"What's all this?" asked Dad when he walked through the door.

"I just thought we'd have a nice dinner," I said.

"To celebrate vacation?"

"Um, yes."

"Well, this is lovely."

"The food's all ready," I told him. "Hamburgers and salad and peas." The peas were from a can, but whatever.

I waited until my father was almost done eating before I said, as planned, "Dad, Kristy asked me something last night."

"Did she? What did she ask?"

I drew in a slow breath. "She wanted to know if I could baby-sit at the Pikes' with her. Next week."

My father put his fork down and rested it carefully near the edge of his plate. "She wants you to baby-sit?"

"With her."

"Mary Anne, no. You are not old enough to baby-sit."

I was ready to pounce. "I'm the same age as Kristy and *she* baby-sits."

Dad paused, but only momentarily. "Kristy's had more experience than you. She has a little brother."

"But how am I going to get experience if I don't start somewhere? And who," I went on, determined to keep the conversation going, "better to start with than an experienced sitter? We'll be sitting *together*."

"No," said my father. "And as for you and Kristy being the same age, that may be true, but there are degrees of maturity to be considered."

I remained calm. "Are you saying I'm immature? Because my teachers always say that I'm very conscientious. And mature. *Ma*-ture. They said so on my last report card. The one I just got. Remember?"

"Well, that's true. Your teachers have always found you to be responsible and reliable."

"Those would be good traits for a sitter, don't you think?"

Dad had to agree that a good baby-sitter would be responsible and reliable.

"I'm going to be in seventh grade this fall," I pointed out. "Kristy sits and Claudia sits. Couldn't I try it, too?"

Dad mulled this over while I sat on my hands, the picture of control and assurance. At last he said, "All right. You may baby-sit with Kristy provided that you're home by nine, that you check in with me every half hour . . ." On and on. Dad made up quite a few rules on the spot.

But I didn't care. I had been given permission to baby-sit! I couldn't wait to call Kristy.

[3] CLAUDIA

The morning was gloomy and wet and windy.
I never minded a day like that, though. That was
because one of my favorite places in the world
was my bedroom. In my room I could entertain
myself for weeks, maybe months, if I had enough
art supplies. And Nancy Drew books. And junk
food. So the weather didn't bother me.

It didn't bother my older sister, Janine, either.
Janine the Genius cared only about her summer
school classes — unlike most normal fifteen-
year-olds, she was taking summer school classes
voluntarily, because she *liked* them. I once heard her
say, "School is my world, math feeds my soul." So
as long as Mimi could drive Janine to the community college (yes, she was already taking classes at
college), my sister was content.

On that damp late-June Monday, Janine was
happily at school and I was happily in front of the
easel in my bedroom. A bag of M&M's lay open
at my elbow. I was trying to concentrate on the
painting I was working on for art class, but what

was really on my mind was my birthday, which was coming up in less than two weeks.

I needed to plan my party. And I wanted to do it on my own, without outside interference—in other words, without suggestions from my parents. We were going to have very different ideas about my party this year. For the past I-don't-know-how-many birthdays, I'd held a sleepover party, inviting Kristy, Mary Anne, and three or four other girls. I knew that was what my parents expected I would do this year, too. Mom and Dad were creatures of habit, and my dad frequently said, "If it ain't broke, don't fix it." (To which Janine would reply, "I suppose that sometimes it's acceptable for one to use *ain't* as the colloquial contraction for *is not*. . . ." Blah, blah, blah. Before she'd finished the sentence, I'd stopped listening.)

Anyway, I had a different—very different—idea for my party this year. I was dreaming of a boy-girl pool party. We didn't have a pool, but our next-door neighbors the Goldmans did. (Why is it you say "Goldmans" and not "Goldmen"? Oh, well.) The Goldmans were very generous and frequently offered us the use of their pool. So I was hoping that they might allow me to have an afternoon party in their backyard. That wasn't the main hurdle, though. The main hurdle, party-wise, was the idea of inviting boys. Not that the

Goldmans would care. No, it was my parents, and probably Janine and Mimi, too, who would have something to say about boys.

I could hear it already.

Dad: But, Claudia, you're only eleven.

My response to this would be that I was eleven *now*, but I was *turning* twelve.

Mom: But you've always had a sleepover.

Me: I can't have sleepovers forever.

(I would refrain from saying "You don't have sleepovers on *your* birthday.")

Mimi: Are you certain this is what you want to do, my Claudia?

(Mimi's objections were always gentler than anyone else's.)

Janine: But *I* haven't even had a boy-girl party.

(I would really have to hold my tongue here if I didn't want to spoil my chances of being given permission.)

I was *so* different from everyone else in my family. I mean, I knew everyone was different. That was what grown-ups always said, usually to make you feel better about something, like the fact that you'd gotten another bad grade. "Well, everyone is different, Claudia. You have your art. . . ." (My guidance counselor said this as she scanned my most recent report card.) But I happened to think I was *more* different from the rest of my family than they were from each other.

Mom and Dad and Mimi and Janine were all prim and proper and conservative and serious. And then there was me. I wore outfits that left them scratching their heads, and I sat in my room and painted or gave myself new hairstyles while they worked or studied. My supreme lack of concern over my grades was nearly unfathomable to them (as unfathomable to them as Janine's interest in grammar was to me).

So my desire to have a boy-girl swim party instead of a girls-only sleepover was going to come as — well, maybe not as a shock, since, after all, my family had lived with me for nearly twelve years. But it was going to be met with resistance.

I put down my paintbrush and picked up a pen. Resistance or not, I intended to invite boys to my party. I decided to make up the guest list. I could show it to my parents when I told them about the party, in order to demonstrate how much preparation I'd already done. They would see that I was serious.

I found a pad of paper and headed it: GEUST list. Then I wrote BOYS on one side of the paper and GRILS on the other. Under BOYS I scribbled Pete, Rick, Howie, Kurt, Darnell. Under GRILS I wrote Dori, Emily, Polly, Kristy, Mary Anne.

I was just thinking how much younger Kristy

and Mary Anne seemed than everyone else on the list when I heard voices downstairs, and then Mimi called to me, "Claudia? Kristy and Mary Anne are here."

I had barely enough time to shove the list in the desk drawer before Kristy, who was fast on her feet, appeared in my doorway. Mary Anne was right behind her, and her arms were full of dolls.

"Hi!" said Kristy and Mary Anne in unison.

"Hey," I replied.

"What are you doing?" asked Kristy.

I gestured to the canvas on my easel.

Mary Anne dropped the dolls on my bed and leaned in for a look. "Ooh, Claudia, that's beautiful," she said.

"Thanks," I replied modestly. I was rather proud of my current painting, which was for art class and was of an imaginary landscape.

"Where is that?" asked Kristy, studying the little cabin that was taking shape beside a stream.

"In my head," I answered, and Kristy laughed.

I glanced at my bed. Four nude dolls now lay on it. "Um . . ." I couldn't think how to phrase my question. What I wanted to say was "What are *those*?" But I didn't want to hurt anyone's feelings. Still, here we were, nipping at the heels of twelve, and Mary Anne had just brought four dolls into my room. Finally, I said cautiously, pointing to the dolls, "I haven't seen those before."

"They're Mary Anne's," said Kristy. Then she added, "They need clothes."

"So we thought we'd get advice from you," added Mary Anne.

"Doll advice?" I felt my stomach drop.

"No, fashion advice. The clothes they were wearing were—"

At this very moment, like a rescue helicopter appearing above someone stranded on a desert island, Mimi once again called up the stairs. "Claudia? Girls? I'm going to drive into town. Do you want to come with me?"

I leaped to my feet. "Yes!" I shouted. "Yes, I do!"

Mary Anne glanced at me, and I couldn't quite read the expression on her face. It was somewhere between hurt and puzzled. "I want to go to the shoe store," I said to my friends. "I need . . ." Frankly, there wasn't much I needed in the way of shoes, since that was mostly what I spent my baby-sitting money on. "There's a sale," I finally said. "I just want to look. Maybe there'll be some good bargains. Want to come with me?"

Kristy made a face. "Not really."

"Not really," echoed Mary Anne.

"Claudia?" Mimi called again.

31

"Coming!" I replied.

Mary Anne gathered up the dolls, and as I watched her walk out of my room, her possessions cradled in her arms, I felt a pang of sadness. When, exactly, had I become so different from Mary Anne and Kristy? When had an armful of dolls come to represent the gap I felt widening between us?

"How about if I call you later?" I said to my friends' backs as they reached the staircase.

"Sure," said Kristy.

"I *will* call you," I promised.

There was no response. Still, what I felt as I climbed into the car next to Mimi was enormous relief.

I didn't have to play dolls.

The relief lasted for about two minutes and then was replaced by regret, but I couldn't take back what I'd said, and anyway, the problem wasn't the dolls but Kristy and Mary Anne and the vast differences between us.

"You are very quiet, my Claudia," said Mimi as we drove slowly toward downtown Stoneybrook.

Mimi, my beloved Mimi, came to this country from Japan when she was thirty-two years old. She spoke with a gentle accent. Mimi might have been as proper and conservative and serious as the rest of my family, but she also understood me better than anyone else in the world. I could tell her things that I would never tell my parents or Janine. Or Kristy or Mary Anne.

"I'm just thinking," I said now.

"About Kristy and Mary Anne?"

Now, how did Mimi know that? "I guess."

"Would you like to talk about it?"

"Yes. But I don't know what to say."

Mimi nodded. "Sometimes it is like that. Words don't express the thoughts accurately."

"Especially not when the thoughts are all jumbled," I told her, and stared out the window at the rain.

★   ★   ★

That afternoon the rain stopped and the sun came out. By supper time the air was clear and warm, so I said to Mimi, "Could we eat dinner outside tonight?"

"That's a lovely idea, my Claudia. Why don't you set the picnic table?"

So I did, and later, when Mom and Dad came home from work, my family and I sat at the picnic table while the sun set beyond a row of trees. Janine was glowing from a day of statistics and sentence diagramming, and I felt pretty content myself.

"This is the life," I said, spreading my napkin on my lap and contemplating Mimi's dinner of salad and rice and baked chicken.

My mother smiled at me. "Did you have a nice day? What did you do?"

"Worked on my painting and went downtown with Mimi." I didn't bring up the subject of the party. It wasn't quite the right moment. "How about you?" I asked, looking across the table at Mom and Dad and Janine, who were seated in a row.

"Same old, same old," answered my father, but he didn't look nearly as bored as he sounded. He loved his job, which had something to do with money or finances or . . . something.

"We were very busy today," said Mom, who was the head librarian at our local public library. She was perfect for the job since she loved books and literature and was very organized. I knew she wished I would visit the library more often, but frankly, my collection of Nancy Drew books was bigger than the library's.

"And you?" I said politely to Janine.

"School was quite enlightening," she replied, and that was when I got to hear all about statistics and sentence diagramming.

I was still trying to determine when I should bring up the subject of my party when my mother said, "Claudia, I was thinking today that since your birthday is only about a week and a half away, we ought to buy supplies for your party and, well, I was going to say that we should send out your invitations, but maybe you feel too old for invitations. Maybe you'll just want to phone your friends."

Perfect! This was the opening I needed! "Actually," I said, "speaking of my birthday and, um, speaking of feeling too old, I was thinking that this year I might have a different kind of party."

"Oh?" said Mom, and everyone at the table turned their eyes to me.

I fidgeted with my napkin. "Yes. I was thinking that instead of a sleepover, which I guess I do feel a little old for," (I chuckled in a mature way) "I might have a pool party."

"A pool party? Where?" asked my father.

I pointed next door. "At the Goldmans'. If they don't mind."

"Well, they have been awfully generous with their pool," said Mom. "I think they'd agree to that."

I nodded, then swallowed hard. "Also," I went on, "I thought I'd invite girls *and* boys. I've already written out the guest list," I added.

This was followed by silence. At last it was broken by Janine, who said, "A boy-girl party?" She sounded like I'd just suggested a party where the guests would play with scissors and fire.

"Well, yeah."

"Oh, Claudia, I don't know," said Mom.

"But I'm turning twelve. And it would be an afternoon party, not a nighttime party. And you

35

and Dad and Mimi would chaperone. Of course you would. And," I went on, "Janine, you could invite a couple of *your* friends. That would be really, um, fun." I looked around at my family, quite pleased with this inspiration.

"Well . . ." said Janine.

"No more slumber parties?" asked Mom sadly.

"I'm sure I'll have plenty more slumber parties. I just thought this birthday could be different."

"I think the swimming pool party sounds lovely," Mimi spoke up.

"You do?" I said. This was going much better than I had imagined.

"It sounds as though you've given this some careful consideration," said Mom.

My father nodded. "We'll have to talk to the Goldmans first, though," he said.

"I know. We can have the party whenever it's convenient for them. It doesn't have to be on my actual birthday."

And that was how my parents agreed to let me have a boy-girl pool party to celebrate my twelfth birthday. I still felt like an elephant in a family of mice, but so what. I decided not to dwell on that. Or on whatever was happening between Kristy and Mary Anne and me. I would concentrate on the party.

I couldn't wait to turn twelve.

4 stacey

This is what I saw when I looked out my bed-room windows: treetops. Would it surprise you to learn that I lived in New York City? Most people who don't live in a city think there are no trees or bushes or wildlife in cities, but that's just not true. I could see Central Park from my bedroom.

Okay, I know that's not the same as having trees in your very own yard, but still. Considering I lived in a giant apartment building in the middle of one of the largest cities in the world, a tree-top view was pretty special. I never took it for granted.

In fact, there wasn't much I did take for granted, and that was because of what happened last year in sixth grade.

I stood at my window and gazed down at the view. The truth was that while I could see tree-tops, I could also see, far below, taxicabs and city buses and an entrance to the subway sta-tion. And if I'd opened my window I would have been able to hear car horns and fire sirens and the grinding of garbage trucks. With the window closed, all I could hear was the humming of my air conditioner. Late June could be sweltering in New York.

I had lived in the Big Apple my entire life and I was going to be sad to leave it behind. But I would not be sad to leave certain people behind. Like everyone in my school, especially Her Royal Meanness, Laine Cummings.

I didn't know exactly how things had gone so wrong, but I was pretty sure that my diabetes was not the cause. It was more of a symptom. Which was kind of ironic—a disease being a symptom of a nonmedical problem. Sometimes I tried to blame the diabetes for what had happened between Laine and me, since that was easier to believe than what had actually happened—that Laine had turned on me. My best friend. Turned. On me.

And now my parents had decided to move. We were going to move away from the city, the only home I'd known, to a very small town that I'd never even heard of. Stoneybrook, Connecticut.

What was I supposed to do in a town without skyscrapers or subways, without movie theatres on every corner or a million restaurants beckoning customers with their fancy menus? On the other hand, what did I care? Stoneybrook would be my chance to start over. With any luck, I wouldn't run across another Laine Cummings.

"Stacey?" my mother called from the kitchen. "Come get breakfast."

I sighed. I wasn't hungry. But I didn't have a choice about eating, not since last fall. That was when I had been diagnosed with diabetes. I thought about saying "I'm not hungry," but I knew where that would get me. I turned away from my window, walked down the hall, and entered our little kitchen.

"'Morning, honey," said Mom. She was at the stove. "I have eggs and sausage for you." I knew she meant organic eggs and meatless tofu sausage.

"Thanks," I replied. I carried my plate into our dining room and sat by myself at the table. A long day stretched ahead of me. Dad was at work and Mom would probably be busy getting ready for our move. Even though we weren't going to move until August, there was a lot to do. The entire apartment needed to be packed up. But sur-prise—even if we brought every last thing in the apartment with us—right down to melted candle stubs and rusted safety pins—our possessions still wouldn't fill the rooms of the house Mom and Dad had bought in Connecticut. So Mom was busy looking for more furniture, plus things we'd never had any use for in New York, such as snow shovels and a lawn mower, all to be sent ahead to our new house. Mom had also decided that now was the time to get rid of things we didn't need anymore (the melted candle stubs, the rusted safety pins). In other words, she had embarked on a massive cleaning out of the apartment.

It was not the most glamorous summer of my life.

I finished my breakfast, paced around the quiet apartment for a minute or two, then finally said to Mom, "I'm going out."

"Okay." My mother was standing in front of a jam-packed closet, obviously trying to decide which things would come with us to our new house and which could be tossed. "Check in later."

It was funny. Where my diabetes and my health were concerned, Mom watched me as if I were two years old. Otherwise, she gave me quite a bit of freedom. I was allowed to walk around our neighborhood on the Upper West Side by myself. I was even allowed to take cabs and buses and the subway on my own, depending on where I was going.

I let myself out of our apartment and walked down the hall to the elevator. In the last few months I'd grown accustomed to doing most things alone. No more meeting friends after school. No more shopping with Laine. I went to the movies by myself and shopped by myself and, until school ended, did my homework by myself.

I rode the elevator to the ground floor and walked through the lobby to the front desk.

"'Morning, Stacey!" Will greeted me. Will was the 8:00 A.M. to 4:00 P.M. doorman. He'd known me since I was three, which was when we'd moved to this building from a building downtown in Greenwich Village. It was possible that, at the moment, he was my best friend. "It's hot out there," he informed me.

"Tell me about it," I replied. I could feel a blast of boiling air as Will held the door open for me. "Want anything?" I asked him. "I could bring you a coffee or something."

Will grinned. "No, but thanks for asking."

The day ahead of me was officially empty. I didn't even have an errand to run.

I walked along Broadway for a block or two, looking into store windows. I walked by a movie theatre to see what was playing. Finally, I walked over to Riverside Park, where I plunked myself down on a bench to do some people-watching. An old man and an old woman were sitting at the other end of the bench, sharing a sticky bun and talking quietly. A group of toddlers hustled by, two by two, with their day-care teachers, everyone joyfully singing "This Old Man."

Three girls my age ran into the park, arm in arm, laughing and calling to a group of boys who were playing catch. I didn't know any of them, the boys or the girls, but I felt a pang as I listened to their easy chatter and watched the girls toss their hair as they approached the boys.

Way back last summer, before sixth grade, I could have been one of those kids. Laine and I and one or two other girls from school used to meet up and walk to the park, laughing and talking and whispering secrets, often with a nanny or a parent hovering in the background. They'd felt like my sisters, those girls, which had been very satisfying for an only child. Our phone rang constantly then, and my life was full of plans and meetings and excursions.

But that changed as soon as sixth grade started, shortly *before* I got sick. Laine had gone away to summer camp in Maine for the month of August. When she'd returned, she was different. My best friend, Laine Cummings, was on her way to being crowned Her Royal Meanness.

Here's a fact about Laine and her family and me and my family: Our parents were best friends before Laine and I were old enough to say "goo-goo, ga-ga," and they were *still* best friends. Of course, they were delighted when Laine and I, as little girls, became best friends, too, but when

Laine turned into Her Royal Blah-Blah, the best-friend situation became a bit complicated. Laine and I might not have been speaking to each other, but our parents were still yapping on the phone, planning dinners and outings and trips to the theatre.

The beginnings of the change in Laine were subtle, as subtle as the first signs of my diabetes. Laine returned from Maine a week before sixth grade began. I expected her to phone me the exact moment she walked into her apartment. I wanted to hear everything, every detail about camp—about bunk mates and counselors and campfires and whether the girl campers ever snuck out to see the boy campers. I hadn't been to overnight camp, and my knowledge of such an adventure was limited to having watched *The Parent Trap*—with Laine, of course.

Mrs. Cummings had told Mom that Laine would be dropped off at their apartment building by the camp bus at three-thirty that afternoon. So at 3:25 I plunked myself down by the phone and waited for it to ring. When it hadn't rung by 3:35, I decided that Laine's month's worth of camp clothes probably stunk, and that her mother had made her unpack her trunk first thing. But the phone didn't ring by four o'clock and it didn't ring by dinnertime. Finally, not long after Mom and Dad and I had finished eating supper, I decided to call Laine. The only reason she hadn't called me by that time, I told myself, must have been because she was sick.

"Laine! How are you?" I cried when she picked up the phone. "Are you okay?"

"Hi, Stacey. Of course I'm okay. What do you mean?"

"Well, I—I just thought—I guess I meant— you didn't call when you got home—"

"Well, I've only *been* home for three and a half hours," she said. And that was when I detected the first nasty hint of . . . something. Something in her tone.

But then the rest of the conversation was okay. Eventually, Laine did tell me everything about camp. And when we finally hung up the phone, I told myself I'd been silly to think that anything was wrong. But *then* the entire next day went by without a word from Laine. Before she went to camp one of us would have called the other first thing in the morning and we would have made our plans for the day. I suppose I could have called Laine, but an unfamiliar voice was twittering around in my head, telling me that Laine would be annoyed if I phoned her.

Annoyed? Laine? The person I thought of as my sister? But I listened to the voice and didn't call her until the next day. By then I couldn't stand it any longer. When I did call, Laine seemed surprised to hear from me. Surprised, and a little annoyed.

"Look, I only have a few days to get ready for school, Stacey. I have a lot to do."

I wasn't sure what, exactly, she had to do, but since we always did everything together, I replied, "Well, great. I have stuff to do, too. Want to go shopping?"

There was a pause, after which she said, "I'm going shopping with Kelly."

"Great. I'll meet you."

"We, um, we don't know when we're getting together yet."

I don't think I need to replay the entire conversation for you. You get the idea. That was the way sixth grade began. Laine didn't do anything horrible at first. In fact, it was more what she didn't do: She rarely called me, she didn't save a seat for me in the cafeteria, she didn't stop by with her books so we could do our homework together. And I noticed that none of the other girls did, either. I was on my own. But why? What had I done?

Somewhere in all of this I began to realize that I didn't feel very well, and not long after that I was diagnosed with diabetes, which is a syndrome that has to do with your body's metabolism. My pancreas wasn't processing sugar properly, and that was affecting the amount of insulin in my body. If left untreated, I could get really sick. Luckily, diabetes, even an extreme case like mine turned out to be, can be fairly well managed through diet, exercise, and injections of insulin. Still, I got off to a difficult start, including several stays in the hospital, and my parents were freaking out.

It didn't help that not long before I was diagnosed, they'd found out that they couldn't have any more children, so they began to pay an awful lot of attention to the one they already had. Since that kid was sick, they morphed into these overprotective, super-vigilant people I barely recognized, who monitored every second of not just my meals and my doctor appointments but my life. And, somewhere along the line, they decided that they could protect me further by keeping my diagnosis a secret. I knew they meant well, but they had definitely not thought things through. When Freda Staples, a girl in one of the fifth grade classes that year, was diagnosed with leukemia, she and her parents talked to her classmates about it, and that class became very close-knit, and the kids were supportive of Freda as she went through her treatments.

My parents had a different idea, one that I came to think of as the Silent Treatment. Tell no one. If no one knows what's going on, no one will treat you any differently. Wrong. It was a very,

very bad idea. Since things had already soured between Laine and me, and as Laine became the ruler of the girls in our class, it did not help at all that I had to go to the school nurse frequently, or that I fainted in school a couple of times. But the very worst moment came one night when all the girls in my class (including me — they hadn't resorted to a total freeze-out) were at a slumber party, and Laine and I were sharing a bed. At some point during the night, I wet the bed. That happened sometimes, back when I was a diabetes newbie. But as you can imagine, it did nothing to help the situation with Laine and me. In fact, it was the beginning of the end.

By the time sixth grade was *finally* over, we were officially enemies. And I was officially glad to get the news that we would be leaving New York City, since I was officially tired of spending every second of my life alone. How could a place called Stoneybrook be worse than my life in NYC?

After people-watching in the park for a few more minutes, I turned my attention once again to the giggling girls, gazing after them longingly, and finally headed back to our apartment. The afternoon dragged on. I helped my mother clean out our storage space in the basement of the building. When we were finished, she dusted her hands off on her jeans and said, "A good job well done! Let's call your dad and ask him to meet us at Sal's for dinner. Doesn't that sound nice?"

"Sure," I said. Sal's was a restaurant two blocks away where we frequently ate dinner. Anything would be better than another stultifying, friendless evening at home.

At six-thirty, Mom and I were seated at a corner table in Sal's, waiting for Dad and having one of our arguments about my diet. I wanted to have a regular ginger ale (even though I knew better) and Mom was insisting I order a diet soda, which in fact she did *for* me when the waiter stopped by with his pad and pen. "A white wine spritzer for me, please, and a diet ginger ale for my daughter."

"Mom!" I exclaimed.

"Stacey, a regular soda is not an option, so I don't want to hear another word about it."

"But I'm not a baby."

"Then make adult decisions. You can't have all that sugar."

I fumed in my seat for a while, and was just moments post-fume when my dad, who was sipping happily at the cocktail he'd ordered when he'd arrived, suddenly waved heartily in the direction of the door.

I turned around to see Laine and her parents entering Sal's, Mr. Cummings waving back to my dad.

I dropped my head and groaned.

48

"Hello, everyone," said Mrs. Cummings. She hurried to our table, hugged my mother, and patted my dad on the back. "Hi, Stacey."

"Hi."

The adults noticed that Laine and I gave each other the frostiest of greetings, eyes averted, barely audible "hellos" on our lips, but no one commented on it. A year ago if the Cummingses had unexpectedly walked into a restaurant where my parents and I were eating dinner, Mom and Dad would have asked them to join us. Now, though, Mom and Mrs. Cummings exchanged shrugs and raised eyebrows, and then Laine and her family were seated six tables away from us. I knew that the adults hoped Laine and I would reconcile before the move to Connecticut, but I didn't see that happening, not while Her Royal Meanness was still on her throne.

Twenty minutes later, my father was paying our bill, and my mother was dragging me over to the Cummingses' table. Mom and Mrs. Cummings talked earnestly for a few moments, glancing once or twice at Laine and me, and then suddenly my mother grinned and exclaimed, "Oh, I think that's a wonderful idea! I'll call you about it tomorrow."

I waited until we were outside and halfway down the block before I said, "What's a wonderful idea?"

My mother's face took on a look of extravagant innocence. "Huh?" she said, as though she had no short-term memory whatsoever. "Oh, nothing." And then she mumbled something about a benefit dinner. "For the, um, dentists . . ."

I let the subject drop. But a very unpleasant sensation was creeping over me, as if I were standing at the edge of the subway platform and had just realized someone was behind me, hands out, ready to push.

5 KRISTY

Addressee Unknown.

I looked down at those words, printed accusingly in red ink on the formerly flawless envelope, and thought about what they meant. *Addressee*—a very, very *im*personal way of refer-ring to the person to whom a letter was addressed. *Unknown*—unidentified, mysterious, unheard of, nameless, anonymous.

Any way you put those two words together and applied them to my father, the result was less than desirable. He was a strange person to whom a piece of mail—my letter—had been addressed. A nameless person. An unheard-of person. And so he hadn't received the letter, and *Addressee Unknown* had been stamped—rather harshly, it appeared to me—over his address, which I had written so carefully in my best cursive.

The letter was bundled in with the other mail I pulled out of our box on a hot Wednesday after-noon, and even though I had written a perfectly nice note to my father, and even though I had remembered a stamp, and my handwriting was lovely and legible, I looked down at the glaring red *Addressee Unknown* and I felt ashamed.

I knew Dad hadn't returned the letter himself. *Addressee Unknown* meant it had never reached him, that he had moved on, which was certainly not my fault. But why couldn't I have a father I could keep track of? Why did writing to him have to be such a drama?

I stuffed the letter in the back pocket of my shorts and told myself that my father knew how to get in touch with *me*, if he was interested. He and Mom must be in some sort of contact. It would have been far worse if Dad had actually received the letter and then had sent it back unopened. But he hadn't received it. He didn't know I'd written to him.

My thoughts didn't console me. I felt like a deflated balloon.

"Kristy? What's that?" David Michael was at our front door, watching suspiciously as I crossed our lawn, Louie at my heels.

"What's what?"

"That thing you're hiding in your pocket."

"What are you, a detective?"

David Michael brightened. "A detective! Hey! I like that. I could be a detective this summer. I'll start with the mystery of you. What's in your pocket?"

I laughed. "You're very persistent. That's a good quality for a detective."

"Thanks. What did you hide in your pocket?"

"Something private."

"What is it?"

"If I tell you it won't be private."

"But a good detective—" David Michael started to say, when (thank heaven) I saw Mary Anne's front door open and she waved to us from her porch.

"Hi, Mary Anne!" I called, drowning out my brother.

Mary Anne, dressed in a yellow-and-white outfit, complete with yellow ribbons at the ends of her braids, jogged into our yard and sat on the front stoop, squeezing between David Michael and me. Louie rested his head on her knees. "Kristy," she said, "if a person fell down the stairs—"

"What person?" I interrupted.

"Oh, maybe a four-year-old girl."

"You mean like Claire Pike?"

"Well—"

"Mary Anne, nothing is going to happen when we sit at the Pikes' tomorrow. I promise."

"How can you promise that? How do you know what will happen? Anything could happen!"

The last time Mary Anne and I had spoken, she had asked me if I knew what to do if a smoke detector suddenly went off. "What's the protocol?"

she said. She actually used the word *protocol*. The day before that, she had said, "What if we were baby-sitting and we heard a funny noise? Outside? After dark?"

I dragged my brain back to the present. "Well, of course, I don't know exactly what's going to happen. But I've baby-sat for David Michael a million times—"

"Not really a million," spoke up my brother.

"—and nothing dire has ever happened."

"I skinned my knee that one morning."

"But what," said Mary Anne, "would you do if he fell down the stairs?"

"It would depend on how badly he was hurt."

"Once I fell down the stairs and I just got up at the bottom and kept on going," said David Michael.

"They were carpeted stairs," I informed Mary Anne, "and he only fell down about three steps. So you see what I mean? It all depends. Anyway, like I said, I don't think anyone is going to fall down the stairs while we're baby-sitting."

"Just because a thing hasn't happened yet doesn't mean it will never happen."

I sighed. I was glad Mr. Spier had given Mary Anne permission to sit and all, but her questions were starting to worry me. And annoy me. I was about to tell Mary Anne that perhaps she would feel better if she focused on something positive, such as dreaming up activities with which we could entertain the Pike kids the next evening, when she leaned around behind me and said, "What's that in your pocket?"

"Why is everyone so interested in my pocket all of a sudden?" I asked crossly.

"Because there's something *in* it and you won't let us *see* it!" replied David Michael.

"Hey, you know what we're going to do tonight?" I said to Mary Anne, desperate to change the subject.

"No. What?"

"We're going to sit outside after dark and watch for meteors. All of us. Mom, Charlie, Sam, David Michael, and me. Won't that be cool?" For one brief instant I thought of asking Mary Anne to join us, but I was looking forward to a family evening, just the five of us Thomases.

"Ooh, good idea," said Mary Anne. "I saw a meteor the other night. It was amazing. This flash of light that streaked across the sky so fast I almost wasn't sure I'd seen it. But I knew I had."

"Meteors are magic," David Michael commented dreamily, and then ruined the moment by casually reaching for my back pocket.

I brushed his hand away. "I'm going to surprise Mom," I announced. "I'm going to make us a special dinner. We can have a picnic supper before we look for meteors."

By the time Mom came home from work, and Charlie and Sam came home from wherever they'd been that afternoon, I had spread a blue-and-white checked cloth over the picnic table in our backyard and had set the table with our plastic plates, the ones with seashells and sea horses on them. Very beachy and summery. Now I was standing in the kitchen, making hamburger patties.

"Can you be our grill master?" I asked Charlie. "We're going to have hot dogs and hamburgers. And maybe someone could make a salad. . . ."

"Someone?" said Mom.

"Well, you know. Not me."

Mom laughed. "I'll be glad to make a salad. While I do that, would you set another place at the table, Kristy?"

"Another? But I already set five," I said, glancing out the window at the table as if maybe I'd made a counting error.

"Watson's on his way over."

"*Watson?*" And just like that, the hungry feeling in my stomach was replaced by a sick one. "I thought we were going to have a family night," I said miserably.

Mom started to answer me—opened her mouth and then closed it—but changed her mind about whatever she was going to say.

I glared at her. "He is *not* part of our family!"

Mom gave me a look that plainly said, "I didn't say he was."

"Maybe he *could* be part of our family," suggested David Michael, clasping his hands together.

"Kristy?" said Mom. "Another place, please?"

I didn't answer her.

Mom sighed and set out the salad bowl.

I stomped off to my room. When I heard a car in the driveway, I peeked out my window. Watson emerged from a gleaming station wagon. A sticker on the rear bumper read PROUD PARENT OF AN HONOR ROLL STUDENT. An honor roll student. That must have been his daughter, Karen, since his son, Andrew, was only three years old. But Karen had just graduated from kindergarten. What kind of school had honor roll kindergarten students? A fancy private one, that was what kind. Rich Watson with his big old mansion and his children in private school.

Since Watson couldn't see me, I made a hideous face out the window at him before slumping back onto my bed.

"Kristy!" Mom called a few minutes later.

"WHAT?"

"Watson's here. Would you please come downstairs?"

I chose not to answer her, but I did return to the kitchen. There was Watson, sitting at the table with David Michael. I was pleased to observe, once again, that Watson was getting bald. Mom would never fall for an old bald guy, I told myself, even though I knew perfectly well that Watson wasn't actually old, just sort of thin-haired. In fact, he was approximately Mom's age.

I studied Watson from the doorway of the kitchen and tried to tally up the things that were in his favor and the things that were not. In his favor, he seemed to be a good father to Karen and Andrew, despite having divorced their mother. Karen and Andrew spent weekends at his house, and he went to all their school programs and parent-teacher conferences (according to my mother). Not in his favor was that he was a stuck-up millionaire snob with gobs of money to throw around like a huge show-off. And that he had an enormous Charlie Brown-type bald head. And the fact that he was dating Mom. And the fact that he had shown up with a box from the most expensive bakery in Stoneybrook. And the fact that he was, at that very moment, explaining the designated hitter rule to David Michael, who looked rapt.

Watson glanced up and caught sight of me in the doorway. "Hey, Kristy!" he said heartily. "Ready for those meteors?" Watson always managed to sound like a dad on an old-timey television show.

I shrugged.

Mom hurried inside, having taken the salad to the picnic table. I looked out the window and could see that the table was now set for six.

"Dinner's ready!" Mom announced.

Watson walked ahead of us, carrying the bakery box.

I watched my brothers and Watson hover around the table, trying to decide where to sit. When Watson finally sat at one end, I grabbed the spot at the other end, on the same side, so he'd be hard to see, and therefore less apt to spoil my meal. Charlie plopped down beside me, Mom sat across from Watson, and Sam and David Michael sat jammed together next to her.

Watson waited until everyone was happily scarfing up their food before he said, "I had a thought."

Just one? I wanted to ask.

"Next Saturday," he continued, "I'm going to need a sitter for Karen and Andrew. I was wondering if you'd be available, Kristy."

I didn't hesitate before replying, "Nope."

"Kristy . . . " said Mom warningly.

"What?" I asked brightly, smiling at her from the other end of the table.

Mom shook her head.

"Um," said Watson. He paused. "You mean, you aren't able to baby-sit, or you don't want to?"

I took a whale-size bite of hamburger. "Don't want to," I said, and a tiny bit of catsup dribbled out of my mouth.

"Kristy," said Mom again.

"I'll do it!" said Sam.

"You will?" Watson looked pleased.

"You're kidding!" I cried.

My brother grinned, oblivious. "It'd be fun," he said, and squirted an additional line of mustard down his hot dog. "I've done some baby-sitting, you know," he added, for Watson's benefit. As if that were the issue.

"Well, that would be fine," said Watson. "Karen and Andrew are looking forward to meeting you. All of you," he added, gazing around the table at my brothers and me.

I looked away. And for the second time that day I felt ashamed.

★　　★　　★

Later, after Watson's dessert had been devoured (I said I wasn't hungry for dessert, although I had to admit that the cookies inside the white box looked awfully good) and the table had been cleared, we set six lawn chairs out in the backyard. We settled into them as darkness fell and turned our eyes to the sky. Slowly, the stars began to appear. The moon was rising, too, and I was about to mention that when Charlie exclaimed, "There's one!" and pointed over the roof of our house.

I looked just in time to see a streak of white light, so fast that, just as Mary Anne had said, I wasn't sure I really had seen it. But then another one shot by and a few minutes later a third.

Reclining in my chair on that magical evening, I should have been thinking about the universe, and the mystery and science of the skies, and how far away stars are, and how tiny individual people are. But instead I was thinking that Watson was practically a perfect father to Karen and Andrew, and that he had shown up for a family activity — *our* family activity — on the very day the letter to my own father had been returned because *my* father was, let's just say, less than perfect.

Watson had ruined my evening.

6 MARY ANNE

"Mary Anne? Are you shaking?" Kristy frowned at me as we hurried across the Pikes' front yard.

"No," I lied. I tried to control myself.

"Okay," said Kristy, "because a good baby-sitter has to take charge. You can't let the kids take charge of you."

We reached the porch and I looked behind me at the sun that was starting to set over the house across the street. I drew in a breath and puffed it out again. Then I checked my watch. We were right on time. That was a professional start for my first sitting job. It proved I was reliable and conscientious. I let relief wash over me. And then I thought about burglars and smoke alarms and ambulances and broken limbs.

Kristy rang the bell.

From the other side of the door came a chorus of "I'll get it!" and "Let me! Let me!" and "No, *I'm* going to get it!"

At last the door was flung open, and I saw that the person holding the knob was Mallory, the oldest of the Pike kids. She shrugged apologetically and glanced at her younger brothers and sisters, all crowded behind her, as if to say, "Children. What can you do?"

"Hi, guys!" said Kristy as she tried to edge inside. "You know Mary Anne Spier, don't you?"

I raised my hand in greeting. "Hi," I said.

From beyond the door Mrs. Pike called, "Kids! Let Kristy and Mary Anne come in!" The eight Pikes, all blue-eyed and dark-haired, parted, and Kristy and I walked between them to the kitchen.

I glanced over my shoulder as we passed and saw sixteen eyes looking back at me. At four, Claire was the youngest Pike. Then there was Margo, who was six; Nicky, who was seven; Vanessa, who was eight; the identical triplets — Byron, Adam, and Jordan — who were nine, and Mallory, who was ten. Suddenly, they looked more like a mob than an innocent bunch of kids.

"Thanks for coming," Mrs. Pike was saying. "Mr. Pike and I will be back by eight-thirty. There are cold cuts in the fridge if you want to make sandwiches for supper. You could also make macaroni and cheese. There's milk and juice and, well . . ." Mrs. Pike waved her hand vaguely. Kristy had told me there were not a lot of rules at this house.

"Mrs. Pike," I began, squaring my shoulders,

"could you please show us where the emergency numbers are?"

She indicated a bulletin board on which was posted a sheet of paper listing everything from the kids' pediatrician to the number for Poison Control.

My dream come true.

"Thank you," I said.

Mr. Pike hurried down the stairs then, and in a matter of moments he and Mrs. Pike left.

Kristy and I were on our own.

With eight kids.

The very first thing Kristy did that evening showed me what a brilliant baby-sitter she was. "Mallory," she said, "you are going to be the deputy sitter this evening, since you're the oldest and Mary Anne and I might need some help."

Mallory, who had been hanging back behind her younger brothers and sisters, looking, I thought, a bit sheepish (after all, she was barely two years younger than Kristy and I), grinned. "Really?"

"Sure," replied Kristy. "Now," she continued, "we might as well eat dinner first. Then we can play until your parents come home."

"We don't have to go to bed while you're here?" piped up Nicky, and one of the triplets jabbed him in the side.

"Don't remind her!" said Jordan under

his breath. Or it might have been Adam. Or Byron.

"Hey, it's summer vacation," Kristy told the kids. "Anyway, your parents will be back in time to put you to bed. We get to have fun until then."

"Goody," said Margo. "Want to see my new shoes? They have pink swirlies on them."

"I do want to see them," said Kristy, "but let's eat first. What do you guys want for dinner?"

"Sandwich," said Byron.

"Sammich," said Claire.

"Macaroni," said Nicky.

"Oreos," said Margo.

"Chicken," said Adam.

"Steak," said Jordan.

"Is there Jell-O?" asked Vanessa.

"I'll have whatever's easiest," said Mallory.

"Why don't we have a smorgasbord?" I suggested, and Kristy beamed at me.

"Excellent idea, Mary Anne," she said.

Kristy began pulling items out of the Pikes' refrigerator — bread, cold cuts, mayonnaise, mustard, relish, yogurt, a jar of olives, apple juice, milk, anonymous Tupperware containers, and mysterious packages wrapped in wax paper. She arranged them on the counter while Mallory and I set out forks and spoons and cups and napkins.

65

"Okay," said Kristy. "Go to it, guys." She handed each Pike a plate, instructed the kids to form a line, and immediately and expertly broke up a fight over who got to be first in the line by announcing that she had noticed a bag of M&M's in the cupboard and that she would get it out for dessert, but only if Everyone Behaved.

I looked on, amazed. And feeling useless. Until Nicky needed help opening a bottle of juice, and Margo needed help deciding what to eat since we wouldn't allow her to have Oreos for dinner, and Claire needed help spreading mayonnaise on her sammich. Suddenly, I was a baby-sitting octopus, twisting off lids, making sandwiches and decisions, wiping up spills, and retrieving forgotten items from the counter.

When at last Kristy and I and the kids were seated around the table with our strange meals (Vanessa, for instance, was eating cereal and chicken), I realized that I felt extremely grown-up. I glanced at Kristy and grinned at her.

At the other end of the table one of the triplets (I would have to ask Kristy how to tell them apart) jammed a piece of some sort of meat into his mouth and said, "Let's play Tail Trail."

"What's Tail Trail?" asked Kristy.

"It's actually a really fun game," spoke up Mallory. "You pick a category—"

"We usually choose either food or animals," interrupted another triplet.

"—and you name something that belongs in that category. Like lion."

"If the category is animals," said Nicky.

"And then the next person has to name an animal that begins with the *last* letter of that word. So he would need to name an animal that begins with *N*. And you keep going around the table that way."

"You can't repeat an animal," said Vanessa. "And if you can't think of anything, then you have to drop out of the game. The last person left is the winner."

"It's harder than it sounds," added Mallory darkly.

I didn't see why, so I said cheerfully, "That sounds like a fun dinnertime activity. Let's play." Then, deciding to take charge, I added, "Claire, why don't you start?"

"I'll start, but I won't be able to finish," Claire replied, and I noticed tears brimming in her eyes.

"Why not?" I asked. "I mean, why won't you be able to finish?"

Claire glared at me. "Because I can't spell."

Oh. Duh. Dumb baby-sitter mistake #1: Ask a four-year-old to play a spelling game. I remained calm, though. "All right," I said. "Then you and I will be a team. How's that?"

"Okay!" Claire grinned.

Then Kristy added diplomatically, "Um, is there anyone else who might want to play on a team?" She tried not to look directly at Margo.

"Me! I want to be on your team, Kristy!" exclaimed Margo.

So that was settled.

I turned to Claire. "Okay. You begin. Name an animal."

"Dog," said Claire. She looked at Vanessa, who was sitting on her right.

"Giraffe," Vanessa said, and looked at Nicky.

To my surprise, Nicky frowned mightily and said, "See? See? That's the problem with this stupid game."

"What?" I asked. So far the game seemed to be going just fine. But, Nicky was staring at his plate, so I glanced helplessly first at Kristy, who shrugged, and then at Mallory.

"The problem is that a lot of words end in *E*," Mallory informed us.

"Like *giraffe*," muttered Nicky.

"And it gets really hard to keep coming up with animals that *start* with *E*," Mallory continued. "But, Nicky, this is only the first one. You can think of an animal that starts with *E*."

"An *obvious* one," said one of the triplets, rolling his eyes.

Nicky brightened. "Elephant!" he exclaimed.

"Turkey," said a triplet.

"Yak," said another triplet.

Margo looked questioningly at Kristy. "Crow?" she suggested, and was met with a chorus of hoots from the boys.

"Good try," said Kristy, ignoring the hoots. "*Crow* sounds like it starts with *K*, but it actually starts with *C*. We need an animal that starts with *K*."

"Is a kayak an animal?" asked Margo. (More hooting.)

"No, although it does start with *K*," Kristy told her.

The letter *K* stumped everyone briefly and then the game continued. Very quickly, however, the *E* issue became a problem, especially after we had used up *ermine* and *elk*. One by one we began to drop out of the game. Animals beginning with *N* were becoming a problem, too, but Byron (I was pretty sure it was Byron) saved himself in a rather spectacular manner near the end of the game by coming up, at the last possible moment, with a triumphant "Naked mole rat!" which all the Pikes assured Kristy and me was a real animal. Eventually, Byron won the game.

When Kristy proclaimed him the Tail Trail Champion, I noticed tears brimming in Claire's eyes again, so, since dinner was over anyway, I said brightly, "Time for M&M's!"

I was rewarded with a grateful smile from Kristy.

After the M&M's had been devoured, Kristy and I cleaned up the kitchen ("A good baby-sitter never leaves behind a mess," Kristy informed me), and then Nicky said, "Who wants to go outside and play softball?"

"Me!" shouted the triplets.

"Not me!" shouted Claire, Margo, Vanessa, and Mallory.

Completely forgetting that just an hour earlier I had been shaking as I walked to the Pikes' house, I now said, "Kristy, why don't you go outside with the boys, while the girls and I . . ." Here I hesitated. "While we . . ."

"Play Beauty Parlor?" suggested Margo.

"Yes! While we play Beauty Parlor."

And that was how Kristy and I spent the next hour of our baby-sitting job. Kristy, who's an excellent softball player, organized some sort of game with the boys in the Pikes' backyard, while I braided the girls' hair and showed them how to make jewelry out of pipe cleaners.

No one fell down the stairs.

And no one needed first aid of any sort, no strangers came to the door, the smoke detector didn't go off, the phone didn't even ring. I could hardly believe it when Mr. and Mrs. Pike suddenly walked through the door. By then it was growing dark, and Kristy and the boys had come back inside and all ten of us were making pipe cleaner jewelry.

I'd been so excited about baby-sitting that I had actually forgotten that I would get paid for doing it. When Mrs. Pike opened her wallet, took out some bills, and folded them into Kristy's and my hands, I almost said, "What's this?" Which, of course, would have been dumb baby-sitter mistake #2, but I caught myself in time. I did, however, say "Whoa!" under my breath, and Kristy gave me a strange look.

"You've done a wonderful job, girls," said Mr. Pike. "The kitchen is as clean as a whistle."

"And we're all in one piece," spoke up Claire, which made her parents laugh.

Mr. Pike drove Kristy and me home then. I thought we could have walked, since it was only a couple of blocks, but I also knew my father would have a fit if he found out we'd been ambling around the neighborhood after dark.

"Thank you, Mr. Pike!" I called as I ran to my house. "'Night, Kristy! See you tomorrow."

I burst through my front door and found Dad in the living room, reading the paper. He was sitting on the couch, which probably meant he had been watching for me out the window.

I thrust my money toward him. "Look!" I said. "I earned this myself! And everything went really well." (Dad already knew this because of my check-in phone calls.) "Kristy taught me about being in charge, and lots of other things. Kristy is an expert, Dad." I stopped to draw in some air. "And the kids really liked me, I think. I played Beauty Parlor with the girls. I was responsible and reliable, and also creative."

Slowly, Dad started to smile. "Mary Anne, I'm proud of you."

"Really?"

"Of course."

"Do you think I might baby-sit again?"

Dad folded his newspaper into a tidy rectangle. Before he could open his mouth to answer, I said, "Please, please, please?" realizing that I sounded the opposite of grown-up.

"Yes. You may baby-sit again." (I refrained from jumping up and down.) "But I'm going to set some ground rules."

Ground rules. Huh. "Okay . . ."

"You may not baby-sit unless you're teamed up with another sitter."

"Even if I'm just sitting for one kid?"

"Even if you're just sitting for one kid. You must be home by nine o'clock if you're sitting at night. You have to make sure . . ."

The rules went on and on until finally I said, "I thought you were proud of me."

My father looked surprised. "I am. I said I was."

"But you sound so . . ." My voice trailed off, and I frowned. This was no time to be at a loss for words. I cleared my throat. "I don't mean to be rude, but it feels like you're telling me I can baby-sit and treating me like a little kid at the same time."

I watched Dad closely, trying to gauge his reaction to my words. *Had* I been rude? I honestly wasn't sure. He picked up the newspaper, glanced at it, and then set it on an end table, so that the corner of the paper was aligned with the corner of the table.

"Mary Anne," he said at last, "I suppose there's a fine line between protecting you and babying you. Maybe, in fact, I'm overprotecting you. But you're all I have. And so I must ask that you respect my rules."

"Oh, I do. I do respect them, Dad." I leaned down and pecked him on the cheek. (We're not very huggy people.) "Thank you for letting me baby-sit. I'm going to be an excellent sitter. You'll see."

I walked up the stairs to my room, thinking that I, Mary Anne Spier, had just become a baby-sitter.

7 CLAUDIA

On my twelfth birthday my parents gave me a necklace, this shirt I'd been dropping hints about for three or four weeks, and a gift card for the art supply store. Janine gave me a book I knew I'd never read, so I couldn't even really say it was the thought that counted, unless it was just the thought of giving me a birthday present, whether I'd like it or not. And Mimi gave me a pin that had belonged to her grandmother. "She would be happy knowing that her great-great-granddaughter was wearing the pin now," said Mimi, and I folded my arms around her and gave her a huge hug.

That was pretty much the extent of my birthday celebration — until three days later when, on a gloriously sunny afternoon, the pool party took place. Boys and all. The Goldmans had been very gracious. They'd lent us their pool, their pool house, and their kitchen, and on top of that, they'd cleared out for the afternoon. "You don't need us old fogies hanging around," Mrs. Goldman had said to me with a smile. "Mr. Goldman and I will spend the rest of the day in town. Have a wonderful party!"

Mom and Dad and Mimi had prepared platters of food, which we were going to carry over to the Goldmans' kitchen.

"What else do you need for your party?" asked Mom wistfully, thinking, I guess, of chairs for Musical Chairs and paper tails for Pin-the-Tail-on-the-Donkey and goody bags filled with whistles and balloons and bubble gum.

"I think that's it," I said. "See? That's the beauty of a pool party. We really just need the pool and some food."

"What are you and your guests going to do all afternoon?"

I shrugged. "Swim and eat."

And the girls would watch the boys and talk to the boys and show off for the boys. And the boys would watch the girls and talk to the girls and show off for the girls.

I planned my pool attire with great care and attention, changing my mind a number of times. My bathing suit—a new bikini—was fine, but I had to make it into An Outfit. I looked through my hats. I looked through my jewelry. I looked through my sandals. I pulled filmy tops and summery pants out of my closet and tried them on over the bikini. I even experimented with making a beauty mark on my cheek with a glop of mascara, but I didn't know what would happen to the glop when I went in the pool, and I didn't want to risk the embarrassment of watching the beauty mark float off of my cheek and onto a raft or down a drain.

My room looked like a department store changing room at the end of a sale, but by the day of my party I had put together the perfect outfit—sophisticated and, I was pretty sure, alluring, yet acceptable to parents. It was complete with jewelry, hair combs, my silver sandals, and the shirt my parents had given me. If I did say so myself, I looked at least fourteen.

Everyone I had invited to the party had said they could come. The boys knew the girls would be there and were very excited. The girls knew the boys would be there and, with the exception of Kristy and Mary Anne, were also very excited. Kristy and Mary Anne, though, had made faces and had wondered what happened to the slumber parties I used to have.

"There'll be other slumber parties," I said, just as I had said to my mother.

My sister, on the other hand, now seemed excited about the pool party, which was a switch from her original reaction.

"Who did you invite?" I asked her early that afternoon. The party was due to start in an hour and I was standing in front of my mirror, once again scrutinizing my pool wear. I was extremely curious about Janine's answer, since my sister had almost no friends.

"Marlene," she replied, and when I raised my eyebrows in the mirror, she elaborated. "She's in my statistics class."

"Ah," I said.

"And Frankie."

I raised my eyebrows again.

"He's in my statistics class, too."

I was surprised that Janine had invited a boy but not surprised that he was in one of her summer classes. So. Janine had invited two of her — well, it wasn't very charitable to think of them as her loser friends, I told myself, but two of her, let's just say, *scholarly minded* friends. That was all right. They could hang out together. As long as they didn't try to correct *my* friends' grammar, we'd be just fine.

"What are you going to wear?" I asked Janine, turning away from the mirror.

Janine looked at me in surprise. "This."

"That? What you have on now?"

My sister was wearing jeans (and I couldn't help noticing that they didn't fit her very well, making her look rather puffy in places where she wasn't puffy at all) and a T-shirt with a picture of Albert Einstein on the front and $E=mc^2$ on the back. Janine looked down at her outfit and then back at me. "Yes."

"All righty," I said.

A few minutes later I saw the Goldmans pull out of their driveway, and a few minutes after that my mother called up the stairs, "Girls! Come help me carry the food next door!"

Everyone in my family scurried back and forth between our house and the Goldmans' with platters of hamburgers and hot dogs, bowls of salad, bundles of silverware, bags of ice, and bottles of soda. By five minutes to three we were ready for the party, and at exactly three o'clock, Kristy and Mary Anne let themselves through the Goldmans' back gate.

"We're here!" announced Kristy.

"Happy birthday," added Mary Anne.

"Remember that we already gave you your presents. On your actual birthday," said Kristy.

Kristy was wearing jeans and a plain white T-shirt. She stripped them off to reveal what I was pretty sure was last year's bathing suit. At least, it fit like a suit would fit someone who had grown three inches since the last time she'd worn it.

Mary Anne then delicately removed her checked pedal pushers and lavender baby doll blouse. Underneath was the pink frilled suit with the mermaid over her left hip that I definitely remembered from the previous summer.

"I wasn't sure I was going to be able to find this," she said. "But I opened my bottom bureau drawer a few minutes ago and there it was."

A few minutes ago! Had Mary Anne given *no* thought to what she would wear to her very first boy-girl party?

"Come on, Mary Anne!" cried Kristy. "I'll race you into the pool."

With a giant splash, my friends cannonballed into the deep end of the Goldmans' pool and came up laughing and sputtering.

"Hi, Claudia!"

"Happy birthday, Claudia!"

I turned around and saw four kids standing at the gate: Emily Bernstein, Dori Wallingford, Darnell Harris, and Pete Black.

"Hi! Come on in!" I called.

Before I knew it, the yard was full of kids, and Mom and Dad and Mimi were bringing the first round of food out to the picnic table. A hill of gifts had risen on a lounge chair.

I was watching Pete study the back of Janine's shirt from afar, a frown on his face, when I heard the gate open again and saw Janine's expression change from bored (she'd been talking to Emily) to terrified to . . . I think the word would be *luminous*.

I turned and followed her gaze to the gate. Approaching it was a boy with a head of dark curls who was at least four inches taller than any of the other party guests. He was whistling, and as he opened the gate he spotted my sister and waved to her.

Janine waved back. "Hi, Frankie!" she called. She abandoned Emily and ran across the yard, pulling me with her. "This is my friend Frankie Evans," she announced. "Frankie, this is my sister, um, my sister . . ."

"Claudia," I supplied.

Frankie grinned at me. "Hey. Happy birthday."

That was it. That was all he said as the gate was closing behind him. So I can't explain what happened next. Maybe it was his grin — who knows? — but suddenly "Happy birthday" took on a meaning of galactic proportions. It was as if Frankie had said instead, "You are a young woman of stunning beauty. Thank you for inviting me into your life." And also, "Why is it that we haven't met before? I know we're destined to be together."

But all I said in reply was, "Thanks."

"Frankie goes to SHS," Janine informed me.

"Well, I *will* be going to the high school. This fall," Frankie told me. "I'll be a freshman."

I couldn't stop staring at him.

"Claudia?" said my sister.

I shook myself. I actually shook myself.

I saw Janine narrow her eyes at me.

Somehow I managed to speak again. I waved my hand around, indicating the backyard. "The food's over there," I croaked. "Help yourself."

"Claudia. He can *see* the *food*," said Janine.

Frankie grinned at me again, which caused me to feel slightly off balance, but before I could say anything to my sister, I heard Rick Chow calling to me from the gate.

"Come on in!" I called back, and managed to drag my eyes and my thoughts away from Frankie.

I was thinking instead how interesting it was to see my male classmates wearing nothing but their bathing suits, when from the direction of the pool I heard Kristy shout, "Marco!" and then Mary Anne's answering shout of "Polo!" At the same moment my father appeared in the yard wearing Mrs. Goldman's apron, which said KISS THE COOK in red letters over a picture of a very bosomy cartoon lady. I barely had time to be mortified, though, because when Janine, who was mortified enough for both of us, saw our father in the apron, she stared at him in horror, took a step backward, and fell in the pool, still fully dressed.

"Janine!" yelled a guest I didn't recognize, so I figured she was Marlene. Marlene was also not wearing a bathing suit, but when she saw Janine in the pool, she jumped in after her, clothes and all. "Hang on to me!" she spluttered, to which Janine replied, "I can swim."

I hovered at the edge of the pool, open-mouthed.

I heard laughter.

Dori was standing next to me. She said, "It could be worse. Remember—I'm the one who got a No-Pest strip stuck in my hair."

I did remember. It had happened in front of our math class and Mr. Conklin had had to cut the sticky strip out of Dori's hair with a pair of pinking shears he found in his desk.

Recalling someone else's embarrassment does help relieve your own, but still. This was not quite what I had envisioned for my party. Especially not when a Greek god had unexpectedly shown up.

After Janine and Marlene had climbed out of the pool and peeled off their wet clothes, and after I had hustled into the Goldmans' kitchen and asked Dad if he could wear *Mr.* Goldman's plain white chef apron—or better yet, no apron at all—the party got back on track. I managed to ignore Kristy and Mary Anne, who remained in the pool and steered clear of the boys. I think Mary Anne was steering clear because she was so shy. She could barely speak to boys in school when they (and she) had all their clothes on. So the experience of seeing them close up, as if in a zoo, with*out* their clothes (or hers) was nearly unbearable. Kristy just thought the boys, clothed or otherwise, were disgusting. I heard her make at least one remark to Mary Anne that included the term "booger breath," and that was when I decided to ignore Mary Anne and Kristy entirely.

I was standing near the picnic table, talking to Dori, when I felt a hand on my shoulder. "Can I fix you a hot dog or something?" said a voice. A semi-deep male voice.

It was Frankie, and he was watching my mother slide another batch of hot dogs onto a platter.

"Um, sure," I replied, trying to ignore the fact that the Goldmans' backyard had started to spin.

Frankie led me to the table, and I actually had to look at my arm to see if his fingers had left some kind of mark there. Why else would my wrist seem to be on fire?

He placed a hot dog in a bun. "Catsup or mustard?" he asked.

"Both," I replied, hoping that didn't seem weird.

"That's how I like them, too." Frankie squirted catsup and mustard onto the hot dog and handed it to me with a flourish.

"Thanks," I said.

"Want to go sit down?" asked Frankie.

Immediately, the yard began to spin again. Maybe I was sick. But no, I had been fine until

Frankie had told me I was a stunningly beautiful young woman. I mean, until he had said, "Happy birthday."

I was following Frankie to a lawn chair (truthfully, I would have followed him into a nest of snakes) when Janine, who doesn't usually like being the center of attention for any reason or for any length of time, suddenly cried, "Hey, Claudia! How about opening your presents?"

Most of my guests were taking a break from the pool and fixing themselves plates of food, and the girls looked with interest at the pile of gifts on the chair.

"Yes, open them!" exclaimed Polly Hanson.

So I hurriedly finished the hot dog and began opening. Frankie sat next to me (now my entire left side was on fire) and helpfully stuffed all the wrapping paper and ribbon into a trash bag. Janine sat next to *him* and kept saying things like, "I remember when *I* was twelve years old," and "Gosh, I haven't seen one of *those* since I was in seventh grade."

Frankie nodded and smiled at her and then brought me a glass of ginger ale. "I put in extra ice cubes," he said.

I finished opening the presents—a fake nose ring (my parents would love that), earrings, a little jeweled mirror, another gift card for the art store—and thanked my friends. Marlene and Frankie hadn't brought me anything, of course, since they didn't know me, but now Frankie said, "I just heard the best new song. I'm going to get it for you. You'll really like it."

"Wow. Thanks," I said breathily. "You don't have to—"

"But I want to."

"Hey, Frankie!" called my sister.

Frankie turned around, and Emily grabbed my hand. "Claudia!" she said in a loud whisper. "He likes you!"

I gripped the arm of the chair. "Frankie does?" I said, and realized I was squeaking. I coughed. "You really think so?"

"It's obvious! It couldn't *be* more obvious. And he's going to be a *fresh*man. You are so lucky. He's *cute*."

I risked a glance over my shoulder at Frankie, who was being led around to the other side of the pool by Janine. "He *is* cute," I agreed.

What an understatement. It was like calling the pyramids cute.

The party continued. Frankie left Janine, sat beside me, and told me about his friends and the fact that they had started their own garage band. I tried to appear as if I were listening instead of thinking of ways to capture his excessive cuteness on paper. Mimi brought out my birthday cake and Frankie helped me cut it. When the air began to cool off, Frankie handed me his T-shirt. It smelled very boyish. In a good way.

The guests began to leave. I walked Frankie to the Goldmans' gate. "Here," I said, and began to peel off his shirt.

He touched my wrist again. "That's okay. I don't want you to be cold. I'll get it from you some other time."

There was going to be another time. Another time with Frankie. That was all I could think about as the best birthday party ever came to an end.

★　　★　　★

The feeling of ecstasy and wonder lasted until that evening.

Mom and Dad and Mimi and Janine and I had cleaned up the Goldmans' house and yard and now were back at our own house. I was in my room, putting away my gifts, and thinking about—what a shock—Frankie. He was the most amazing thing that had happened to me in a long time, and I had suddenly, heartbreakingly realized that there was no way I could talk about him with my two oldest friends. I tried to picture myself having a conversation about Frankie (and spinning yards and wrists on fire) with Kristy and Mary Anne. And I couldn't do it. I kept hearing murmurings of "Marco Polo" and "booger breath." And remembering Mary Anne in her mermaid suit, and Kristy diving underwater to escape Pete Black when he swam too near her.

I felt sad. I felt as though I were walking away from . . . what? From something I might not like but that I knew I was going to miss anyway.

I was trying to sort out my thoughts when I heard my sister's bedroom door slam. I peeked into the hallway. "Janine?" I called.

Nothing.

"Janine?"

"Leave me alone."

"But I didn't do anything."

Janine opened her door a crack, just long enough to say, "Are you kidding me?" She paused. "Think about it." Then she slammed her door again.

Think about what? This was the trouble with a smart person. Janine sometimes thought I knew everything she did. I was about to yell this very thing through her closed door when Frankie floated into my mind again. I was enjoying that pleasant image, when suddenly it was replaced by another one. In this one I saw my sister's face become luminous as Frankie walked through the Goldmans' gate. And all of a sudden I understood.

My sister liked Frankie. And that was why she had invited him to the party.

Uh-oh.

8 stacey

When I was in sixth grade, I started baby-sitting for some of the kids in my apartment building. Thank goodness. If it weren't for those kids, I would hardly have had anyone to say good-bye to when we moved to Connecticut. There were Will and the other doormen, of course. But if my parents and I had moved after, say, fifth grade, I would have had to plan tearful good-byes with Laine and about twenty-five other ten- and eleven-year-olds. Now . . . well, there were Will and Tomas and Nazim and the maintenance crew; and the Beckett twins, who were three; and Twila and Jeremy Rosenfeld, who were five and eight; and the Goldsmith children. But as for anyone my own age? Zippo.

It was mid-July and our apartment was already partially packed up. My mother had finished her grand cleaning out, and we had all been amazed at how much we didn't need. We'd given away boxes and bags of stuff: clothing that didn't fit and things my parents found in closets that we realized we hadn't used in five or ten years. My mother had even discovered a box that had never been unpacked after we had moved out of our last apartment.

"All right," Mom said the very morning after the final bag of unwanted things had been carted away. "Time to start packing."

I was about to reply, "Couldn't we have just one day when we don't have to clean or pack?" but then I realized I didn't have anything else to do except baby-sit, so I dutifully dragged some empty cartons into my bedroom and began filling them with winter clothes.

That afternoon, though, I had a sitting job with Twila and Jeremy Rosenfeld, and I happily abandoned my disheveled room.

"We're playing Sticky!" Twila announced as soon as Mr. Rosenfeld, who was a stay-at-home dad, had left for his dentist appointment.

The Rosenfeld kids, who lived in apartment 15-K, were two of my favorite sitting charges.

"Sticky? What's Sticky?" I asked Twila, the five-year-old.

She and her brother were sitting next to each other on the living room couch. They were sitting so close, in fact, that the left side of Twila's body was mashed up against the right side of Jeremy's.

"This," Jeremy replied. "See? We're stuck together."

"And we have to stay stuck together no matter what," added his sister. "Come on, Jeremy. I need a glass of water."

I watched Twila and Jeremy rise from the couch and somehow manage to remain stuck together from their shoulders to their ankles as they made their way into the kitchen. Amidst much giggling, they hobbled to the refrigerator, and Jeremy removed a pitcher of water. Then they hobbled to the cupboard and Twila found a plastic cup. "Do you want water, too?" she asked her brother. When he nodded, she pulled out a second cup. "You pour," she added.

Jeremy lifted the heavy pitcher with his left hand (his right hand still plastered to his sister) and clumsily poured water into the cups.

I was laughing, and so were Twila and Jeremy, but as soon as they were seated (on the kitchen floor because they had difficulty maneuvering themselves onto chairs while remaining stuck together), I said, "You guys? I have to tell you something."

"What?" said Jeremy, eyes narrowing, instantly suspicious. He paused with his cup halfway to his lips.

I had held off telling my sitting charges about the move until now because I'd learned that little kids have a different concept of time than older people. If I'd told them in May that I was moving in August, it would only have meant three months of wondering when I was actually leaving—and probably fretting and pouting. And so I had waited until the move was just a couple of weeks off before I told them anything.

"Well," I said, joining the kids on the floor, "I'm going to be moving away."

Twila lowered her cup. "Moving away where?"

"To Connecticut. Do you know where that is?"

"In Midtown?" she guessed.

Jeremy unstuck himself from his sister, stood up, and said angrily, "It's not in Midtown! Connecticut is a whole different state. You're moving far away, aren't you, Stacey?"

"Hey, you lose!" crowed Twila. "You came unglued."

"I don't care." Jeremy glared at me.

"Connecticut *is* a different state," I said diplomatically, "but it isn't really that far away. Our new house will be just a couple of hours from here."

Reality began to sink in for Twila. "A couple of *hours*! That's . . . that's . . ." She couldn't think of anything comparable.

"That's *far*," said Jeremy accusingly. "Why are you moving?"

"Because my dad got a new job." That seemed like the simplest answer.

"Our dad doesn't work," commented Twila.

"What does that have to do with anything?" exclaimed Jeremy, but his lower lip was trembling.

"What could I do to make this better?" I asked.

Jeremy stared at the wall and wouldn't answer.

"You could get us presents," said Twila brightly.

I smiled at her.

Things went somewhat better when I told Sean and Sarah Beckett about the move. This was because they were three and didn't quite understand what I was talking about, and also because I had only sat for them a few times and they didn't know me as well as Twila and Jeremy did.

"Will a moving van come?" asked Sean with interest.

"Yup," I replied.

"A big one like I saw yesterday?"

I didn't know Sean had seen a moving van the day before, but I said, "Yes. Huge. It has to be big enough to hold all our furniture and all our clothes and everything in our kitchen."

"All your furniture?" Sarah took her thumb out of her mouth long enough to ask this. "A truck big enough for a couch and a bed?"

"For *two* couches and *two* beds and all our chairs and tables and lamps."

"Wow," she said, and reinserted her thumb.

The rest of the conversation revolved around the van and how we would fit our furniture in it. The twins never even asked where I was going.

The Goldsmith children, on the other hand, burst into tears when I gave them the news. All three of them, and all at once, as if I had pressed a button.

"But why, Stacey, why?" wailed Sami.

"We don't like any other baby-sitters!" cried Eloise.

"Only you!" Nathan suppressed a sob.

The next afternoon I sat for two-year-old Caroline Barkan on the fourth floor. Actually, I wasn't so much a sitter as a mother's helper, since Mrs. Barkan was at home. She was holding a meeting in her apartment and she wanted me to keep Caroline entertained until her guests left.

It was almost six o'clock and the meeting had ended, but several people were still hanging around in the living room when Mrs. Barkan suddenly looked at her watch and said, "Oh! Stacey, you should go. Here. Here's your pay." She pushed a couple of bills into my hand and held the door open for me. I was calling good-bye to Caroline when the door closed on me.

Well. That was weird. I rode the elevator back to my floor, wondering if I'd done something to offend Mrs. Barkan. I opened the door to my own apartment, expecting to hear the sound of packing tape being wrenched from its roll, or of a book-filled box being added to the growing pile of packed boxes in the front hall (this was always accompanied by an exclamation of "Oof" from Mom). But the apartment was silent. And kind of dark. It looked as though all the shades had been pulled down.

"Hello?" I called, feeling a prickle of fear at the back of my neck.

And with that, the overhead lights were switched on and I heard cheering and cries of "Surprise! Surprise!"

I stared.

The living room had been cleared of packing cartons and decorated with balloons and a big string of gold letters that spelled out FAREWELL. A piñata in the shape of a pig (I love pigs) was hanging over the coffee table, and the table was laden with snacks and drinks and pig napkins and pig paper plates and pig cups.

Somehow I took this all in while still standing in the doorway. I'm sure my mouth had dropped open. Slowly, my focus shifted from *what* was in the living room to *who* was in it.

Mom. Dad. Twila and Jeremy (giggling and stuck together along one side). The three Goldsmith kids (each holding a wrapped gift). Several other sitting charges. Almost every girl in my sixth-grade class. Mr. Cummings. Mrs. Cummings.

And Laine.

All those people in the room and my eyes locked themselves on Laine's.

Laine wasn't smiling and neither were her eyes.

But everyone else was laughing and talking, and the smaller kids were jumping up and down.

Twila ran to me and threw her arms around my waist, exclaiming, "Me and Jeremy kept the party a secret for three whole days!"

"Stacey, this is for you!" Eloise Goldsmith thrust her gift at me.

"This is for you, too!" cried Sami.

"And this," added Nathan.

"We put our presents over there," said Jeremy, pointing to an end table on which, I now saw, was a stack of gifts and cards.

I was surrounded by my sitting charges like a football player in a huddle. Laine was watching us, smirking. I saw her glance at Naomi and Caitlin, former friends of mine, and the three of them began to giggle.

"What do you think, honey?" asked my father.

I realized I should have some sort of reaction. And that, all things considered, it should be a happy reaction. I disengaged myself from Twila and the other kids and managed to say, "Thanks, everyone! This is great!"

"Are you surprised?" asked Laine's mother.

"Completely," I replied, which was the honest truth.

"Stacey! Stacey! Open your presents!" called Twila.

Mr. Rosenfeld appeared in the crowd and said to Twila, "Give her a chance to greet her guests. She'll open her presents later."

I stood uncomfortably at the entrance to the living room, wanting to avoid Laine and all my classmates. How on earth had my parents convinced them to come to the party?

As if in answer to my question, Laine pushed her way through the crowd until she was standing at my side. "Nice party," she said, in exactly the same tone of voice in which someone would say, "Ew, look. A snake." (Her parents—and mine—were out of earshot.)

I was tempted to reply, "It was so *charitable* of you to come," but sarcasm didn't work well with Laine, especially when she had been sarcastic first.

So I said nothing.

Laine cocked her head and studied me. "You know why I'm here, don't you?" she asked finally. Before I could answer, she said, "Because my parents made me come. And everyone else is here—everyone who's over the age of

96

eight, that is—because I told them they had to come."

I was sure some sort of threat had been attached to Laine's invitation—that the girls had to come or else . . . or else . . . Well, I wasn't sure or else what, but I could imagine. Or else Laine would shun them, too. Or else, surprise, they would no longer be invited to parties and their phones would stop ringing and they would find themselves as alone as I had become.

Her Royal Meanness had evil superpowers.

Mom and Mrs. Cummings, arm in arm and smiling broadly, now approached Laine and me. Laine immediately underwent a transformation.

"Stacey," Mrs. Cummings said, "we're going to miss you."

"*So* much," added Laine. "We're going to miss you *so* much."

Mom and Mrs. Cummings looked at Laine and me fondly.

"Nope, it won't be the same around here," Laine went on.

The moms drifted off and Laine glared at me.

A thought occurred to me then. "Laine," I said, "are you afraid of me?"

I remembered the look on her face when I had wet the bed at the slumber party. And the look when I had gone into insulin shock in school and the ambulance had had to come for me. Maybe —

Laine snorted. "*Afraid* of you? Are you kidding?"

But I thought maybe I was right.

Allison Ritz, who had joined our class at the beginning of sixth grade, wandered over to us now, along with Naomi and Caitlin.

"You certainly have some interesting friends," said Caitlin, turning to eye the Goldsmith children.

"You know," I replied, "friends come in all ages." I could feel anger bubbling just beneath the surface. "And these kids have been a lot nicer to me than any of you have lately." I drew in a breath. "Maybe you should take a few notes."

"Ooh," said Naomi to Laine and Caitlin and Allison. "Stacey has a temper. Is she mad? Did we make Stacey *mad*?"

Mr. Cummings came by then, holding out a dish of teensy pizzas. Laine, Naomi, Allison, and Caitlin each took one.

"Thank you, Mr. Cummings," Caitlin and Naomi and Allison said dutifully.

"Thanks, Dad," added Laine.

"Stacey?" asked Mr. Cummings, holding the tray out to me.

I was far too nervous to eat. "No, thanks." I tried to smile.

Mr. Cummings disappeared, and Laine

frowned at her friends. "My goodness. Stacey isn't eating. What a surprise. Poor Stacey. I guess she needs lots of extra attention, doesn't she? Everyone, please take a moment to worry over Stacey."

Naomi bit back a smile.

And Allison leaned in and whispered loudly, "Watch out or she might wet her pants again."

This caused wild giggling, and much to my surprise, as I watched my former friends and my former best friend have a giant laugh at my expense, I realized that what I wanted to say to them was not "Get out of my life, you rude shrews" but "Why won't you be my friends? Even if you don't know about my diabetes and don't understand what went on last year, why won't you be my friends? I would be *your* friend."

I was pathetic.

I was temporarily saved from further humiliation by Twila, who once again demanded that I open my presents.

"Stacey?" asked my mother. "Do you want to open your gifts?"

I didn't really. Not in front of Laine and the other girls. But I didn't feel I had a choice. My father cleared a spot for me on the couch and handed me the cards and gifts, and for the next half hour I opened boxes and envelopes and said, "Thank you so much!" and "Oh, this is wonderful!

Whenever I look at this I'll think of you." Except for when I opened anything from my classmates, and then I tried to summon up a bit of enthusiasm (after all, the adults were watching) before saying, "Thanks. This is great."

The party was finally nearly over, the food eaten and the piñata emptied and people starting to leave, when Laine walked by the couch where I was sitting, pretended to trip over my feet, and spilled a glass of Coke down the front of my blouse. The blouse, I should say here, was brand-new, and white. I had paid for it with my hard-earned baby-sitting money.

"Oh! Oh, I'm so sorry, Stacey!" cried Laine. "Gosh, I don't know how that happened. Your feet are so big, they're hard to miss. I guess I'm just clumsy."

Giggle, giggle, giggle from Allison, Naomi, etc.

I had had enough. "Mom?" I whispered as I stood in the kitchen, rinsing my blouse off at the sink. "Laine did that on purpose. You saw, didn't you? That wasn't an accident."

"Stacey, for heaven's sake. Don't be silly. Laine wouldn't do something like that on purpose. And I heard her apologize to you."

"Fine," I said.

I counted up the days until our move, which couldn't come soon enough.

9 MaRy aNNe

The summer was sliding by in that way summers have. One day you're counting up the weeks of vacation and thinking the summer seems endless, and the next thing you know you're seeing ads on television for back-to-school supplies. The first time I heard one of those back-to-school ads I was sitting in the family room with my father and I nearly fell off the couch. It was a warm evening in the beginning of August, and Dad had opened the sliding door to the back porch so that we could hear the crickets and owls over the sounds from the TV. We were side by side on the couch, Dad with the newspaper, and me with a scarf I was knitting, trying to ignore the incredible heat the wool was generating on my bare legs as the scarf trailed down over them.

"What's the matter?" Dad asked as I recovered my skein of yarn and regained my balance.

I pointed frantically at the TV. "Did you hear that?"

Dad shook his head.

"It was an ad for Pen and Ink." Pen and Ink was a chain of stationery and office supply stores.

"Ah," said Dad, clearly not understanding why a Pen and Ink ad should make me fall off the couch.

"The announcer guy was saying it's not too early to buy your *notebooks* and *pens* and *paper* and *organizers*."

Dad frowned slightly.

"The ad showed this really happy father taking his grumpy kids shopping for school supplies. *School* supplies, Dad."

My father finally smiled at me.

"It isn't funny! The summer's more than half over. Way more." I paused. "Kristy's birthday is almost here." I liked school and everything, but who wouldn't want summer to go on and on forever?

"What's Kristy planning for her birthday?" asked my father, completely missing the point about vacation.

"Just dinner with her family. She invited me, too."

Dad nodded and went back to the paper, and I turned down the volume on the TV and set my knitting aside. There was a little problem with Kristy's birthday, and I wanted to think about it. So I thought for a while. And I decided that there wasn't just one little problem, there were several, adding up to a big problem.

Here was the thing: Kristy had decided not to have an actual party for her birthday. This was because the party at Claudia's was still fresh in her mind. All those boys. They were bad enough. But the girls in their outfits—and the presents Claudia had been given . . .

If Dad had asked me to make up my birthday list that very night, I would have written down craft kits, and this set I saw for designing doll clothes, and a copy of *The Lion, the Witch, and the Wardrobe*. Also, I kind of wanted a hamster.

Now, Claudia had gotten jewelry, mostly, and some clothing and accessories. That had not been lost on Kristy and me. Nor had the boys or anything else about Claud's birthday. So after much deliberation, Kristy had decided not to have a slumber party or a gymnastics party or any kind of party. She'd settled on a nice dinner at home.

And then she'd invited me (and Claudia, although Claudia wasn't able to come). That had been fine. I was thrilled to have been invited. Except that Kristy had told her mother she *didn't* want to invite Watson. Or his kids. The message being that this was a family party and Watson and Karen and Andrew weren't part of her family— while I was. Mrs. Thomas had tried to be understanding about this, but Kristy could tell she was hurt, and that had upset Kristy, although not enough to make her change her mind.

As bad as all these things were, they paled in comparison to something else about Kristy's birthday: She fervently hoped her father would remember the day in some way—maybe even that he would show up for the party—and I was pretty sure neither was going to happen. How could Kristy even think this? She hadn't seen her father in years, he lived in California and had very little money, and (she had finally confessed to me) she had secretly written him at the beginning of the summer and his letter had been returned to her.

"So you don't know where he lives?" I had said when she'd told me about the letter.

Kristy had looked uncomfortably at her hands, which were absentmindedly fashioning a chain of clover blossoms as we sat in the grass in her backyard. "Does it matter?" she'd replied. "He knows where *we* live. I mean, he and Mom must be in touch. About money and stuff. So he would know we haven't moved or anything. Plus, he knows when my birthday is. I, um, shouldn't exactly have to remind him about that."

No, I had thought. She shouldn't have to. But her father had a very bad track record when it came to birthdays and holidays, or even just to jotting a few lines on a postcard.

"Dad?" I said now, setting aside my knitting. "I want to get Kristy something really special for her birthday this year."

"You do? That's nice of you, Mary Anne."

I nodded. I couldn't tell Dad *why* I wanted to get her something extra special, but that didn't matter.

"Could you take me shopping on Saturday?" I really wished I was allowed to walk downtown and go shopping with my friends or even go shopping by myself, but that was a no-no. Dad wouldn't let me make the trip into town without a grown-up.

"Sure."

"Good. Thank you. I'm glad I earned all that sitting money." I had baby-sat two more times with Kristy, and what with those jobs and my allowance, my wallet was bulging nicely. "Kristy's kind of like my sister," I remarked to my father.

He put the paper down and gave me his full attention. "You two have been through a lot together," he said. "You were there for Kristy when Mr. Thomas left and through all the changes that came afterward."

"And Mrs. Thomas is like a mother to me sometimes," I added, hoping this wouldn't offend Dad. Sometimes he could be very protective of my mother, even though she'd been dead for my whole life.

But he said, "Just like Mimi has been. You're lucky, Mary Anne, to have Mrs. Thomas and Mimi so nearby. And Kristy is lucky to have you."

★　　★　　★

Later that night, I sat in my room and looked through my mother's box. I had no memories of my mom, but I was comforted by the simple thought that all of the things she'd saved had been important to her. Then I thought of Kristy. She had memories of her father, but he wasn't part of her life, and in fact it felt (to me, anyway) that he didn't particularly want to be part of it. Or maybe that he couldn't be.

I had never known my mother; Kristy had known her father but had lost him. Maybe this was what bound us together as close as friends could be, as tight as sisters. There was one enormous difference between Kristy and me, though. I didn't know what I was missing, and Kristy did. Sure, I watched wistfully as my friends celebrated Mother's Day, as Kristy and her mother talked about things I could *never* discuss with Dad, as Claudia and her mother and Mimi occasionally had a "girls' day out." But it was like watching television. Not quite real.

Kristy, on the other hand, remembered Father's Day celebrations and bedtime stories with her dad and playing catch with him at the park. She remembered riding on his shoulders and being scolded for teasing Louie and learning how to dance, her feet on his. She had years' worth of memories. And now she had . . . I wasn't sure exactly what Kristy thought she had, but from the outside looking in, I would say she had a phone call here and there, a card here and there, and a lot of disappointment. And she didn't ask for much from her father. Really, she just wanted him to remember her, to appreciate her.

I set the box on the floor, climbed in bed, and switched off the light. I'd been giving a lot of thought to Kristy's birthday present, and the very first idea that popped into my head now was for a gift that didn't come from a store. I would think about the store-bought gift later. What had popped into my head at the moment was something called Kristy Day. Huh. Kristy Day. A day on which to celebrate and appreciate Kristin Amanda Thomas. That, I thought, would cheer her up, should she be feeling sad after her birthday dinner.

I liked the idea so much that I thought I'd better make a few notes about it. The only trouble was that once it's lights-out in my room, it's really lights-out. Even during summer vacation. Dad was a big believer in getting enough sleep. So I was forced to make my notes by flashlight. I kept one shoved in the back of my top desk drawer for just such situations. I crept out of bed, listened for a few moments at my door but heard nothing at all, and tiptoed to my desk, where, once I had located the flashlight, I also found a pad of paper and a pen.

Back in bed, I positioned the flashlight on a folded blanket and aimed it at the paper, hoping its beam wasn't bright enough so that Dad could see light under my door. Then I opened the pen with my teeth and carefully wrote across the top of the pad: KRISTY DAY.

I began to make notes:

1. *To be held August 21st.* That was the day after Kristy's birthday, a day on which she might be very, very disappointed.

2. *How to honor Kristy? Parade? Skits? Speeches?* I scratched out *Speeches,* thinking I might be getting carried away.

3. *Who should come?* I wrote down *Claudia, Mariah and Miranda Shillaber,* and *Lauren Hoffman.* Mariah and Miranda (twins) and Lauren had been Kristy's friends originally, and I had gotten to know them through her. Sometimes we sat together in the cafeteria. Kristy would be pleased if they could come to Kristy Day. I paused, then added *David Michael, all the Pike kids, Jamie Newton, Jenny Prezzioso,* the kids for whom Kristy baby-sat.

I sat in bed and wrote for fifteen minutes. By the time I finally turned off the flashlight and went to bed (for the second time), I was feeling quite pleased with the way Kristy Day was taking shape.

★　★　★

On Saturday, Dad went into his office for the morning. After he left, I lined up my mother's dolls on my bed and sat next to them with a big pile of yarn in my lap. I was wondering if I could knit hats and scarves for the dolls, and realizing at the same time that knitting doll clothes would be a fabulous baby-sitting activity — I could spread my love of needlework to my sitting charges — when the phone rang.

"Hello, Mary Anne?" said the caller. "This is Mrs. Newton."

"Oh, hi!"

The Newtons lived on my street, and both Kristy and Claudia occasionally sat for Jamie Newton, who was three years old.

"Mary Anne, I understand you've started baby-sitting, and I was wondering if you'd be able to sit for Jamie next week. I need someone from two-thirty to four-thirty on Tuesday afternoon."

My first reaction was to shriek "Yippee! A real sitting job!" since this was the first time a parent had personally requested me, as opposed to my tagging along on one of Kristy's jobs just to get some experience. But I restrained myself. Also, I remembered my father's rules, and although Mrs.

Newton had phoned and asked for me, I would still have to find someone to come with me on the job. Dad had not relaxed his rule about my sitting alone.

I said in what I hoped was a professional-sounding voice, "Yes, I'm free on Tuesday. And I'd be happy to sit for Jamie. One thing, though." I drew in a deep breath. How to explain this? "Um, well, I just started baby-sitting this summer, and my father" (I was very tempted to say that my father was a Rule Freak who still saw me as a preschooler, but *that* certainly didn't sound professional or confidence-inspiring) "prefers that I have a buddy along when I sit. So I'll just need to see if Kristy or Claudia can come with me."

"Oh," said Mrs. Newton. "Well, I—I was only planning on one—"

"Oh, you'll only have to pay for one sitter," I said in a rush. "Don't worry about that. Could I call you back after I talk to Kristy and Claudia? I promise I'll call you by this evening."

"All right," said Mrs. Newton, but she sounded uncertain, and I couldn't blame her. Two sitters for one little kid? A little kid who might even be napping during the entire sitting job?

"Thank you! Thank you, Mrs. Newton," I said before she could change her mind. "I'll call you back soon."

I hung up then and dialed Kristy's number.

"Hi," I said. "Guess what. Mrs. Newton just called *me* and asked *me* to baby-sit! Isn't that cool?"

"Your first true sitting job!" exclaimed Kristy. "That *is* cool."

"Except," I continued, "I still can't go by myself. Can you come with me? Mrs. Newton needs us on Tuesday afternoon."

There was a little silence at the end of the phone.

"Kristy?"

"I'm busy on Tuesday. I'm sitting for Claire and Margo Pike."

"Oh."

"Hey, maybe I could bring the girls over to Jamie's."

I sighed. "No. That's okay. I'll call Claudia and see if she can come."

"I'm sorry," said Kristy.

"It isn't your fault."

I wasn't eager to call Claudia. I wanted to take the job at the Newtons', but I didn't particularly want to phone Claudia and display my baby-ishness to her, as if she weren't already completely aware of it.

I plopped onto my floor and leaned against the bed. I hadn't seen much of Claudia since her party. Well, that wasn't quite true. What I meant was that I hadn't spent much time with her. I had *seen* her often enough—Claudia and Frankie Evans pedaling away from the Kishis' house on their bicycles, Claudia and Frankie sitting side by side on the Kishis' front stoop, Claudia sliding into the Evanses' station wagon on her way to who-knew-where with Frankie's family to do who-knew-what with them.

Claudia and Frankie.

Frankie and Claudia.

Was Frankie Claudia's boyfriend?

Were you allowed to have a boyfriend before seventh grade?

Were you a total baby if you even had to ask these questions?

I slumped farther down onto the floor, but then I heard Dad returning from work and I jumped to my feet. I decided to forget about calling Claudia. For the moment.

"Dad!" I said, running down the stairs to meet him in the kitchen. "Could we go into town this afternoon? I want to buy Kristy's birthday present."

"Sure," said Dad. "That sounds like fun. Let's have lunch at Renwick's first."

"Yes!" I cried.

Dad and I had a very nice lunch and I told him about Mrs. Newton's phone call. Then I looked in four different stores before I found the perfect gift for Kristy—a baseball jersey on which her name could be stenciled along with any number I chose. The man in the store helped me pick out the style and the color of the letters and the number, and before I knew it I was walking away with a gift-wrapped box for my best friend. I had spent quite a bit of my money, but it was worth it.

Dad drove us home then, and at last it was time to face what I'd been putting off. I had to call Claudia and ask if she could baby-sit for Jamie with me. I was very nervous about making the call, which I knew was not a good thing. Calling someone who's been your friend your entire life should not make you nervous. But when I picked up the phone, I noticed that my hands were sweating.

①⓪ CLAUDIA

My sister was barely speaking to me. My oldest friends in the world still played with dolls and laughed at boys behind their backs. I would have felt really lonely if it weren't for Frankie.

Two days after my birthday party he called. Just to talk. He called me on my own personal line and I spoke to him privately in my bedroom. Okay, so answer me this: How did Janine know he had called? I hadn't a clue, but somehow she did know, because after I hung up the phone I found her waiting for me in the hall outside my room, like a vulture.

"Was that Frankie?" she asked.

"Yes." I was shocked. Maybe my sister had magical powers. That would be important to know.

"Uh-huh," said Janine.

I waited for her to say something else, but she didn't, she just slunk back down the hall to her lair.

Frankie called again the next day, and the day after that he dropped by the house for a few minutes. Luckily, Janine wasn't at home, but her powers kicked right in, because the moment she walked through the door that afternoon she said, "Did you and Frankie have fun?"

Maybe my sister had spies in addition to magical powers.

Frankie and I walked downtown and had sodas at Renwick's. (If our arms accidentally touched, the world began spinning again.) We browsed the music store, and I made an effort to spend as much time looking at the merchandise as I did at Frankie. We took a bike ride. I rode behind Frankie and watched the way his curls blew back and got kind of straightened out by the wind. We sat on swings at the elementary school playground and I noticed the pleasant, sun-warmed boy-smell of his skin.

Every time my phone rang I hoped it would be him.

Apparently, I was the only one in my family who felt this way. Nobody *dis*liked Frankie. But I saw the frown that furrowed Mimi's brow when Frankie appeared on our doorstep, and the looks Mom and Dad exchanged when I closed my bedroom door after my phone had rung. They didn't have to say they thought I was too young to have a friend who was a boy. All right, who was I kidding? They didn't have to say they thought I was too young to be spending time with a boy who was clearly more than just a friend. But I knew that's what they were thinking.

One quiet evening when Janine was off at a study group and Mom and Dad and Mimi were reading in the living room, I was sitting lazily on our front steps—not reading, not even really thinking, just sitting—when I saw a bicycle turn the corner onto Bradford Court. Frankie zipped up my driveway and hopped off the bike.

"Hi," he said casually.

I swallowed a giant lump that had formed in my throat at the very sight of him. "Hi," I replied, and was surprised when the voice sounded like my own.

"What are you doing?"

I shrugged. "Nothing."

"Claudia?" my father called from inside. "Is someone here?"

"It's Frankie," I told him, and led Frankie into our living room.

My parents and Mimi hadn't had much opportunity to talk to Frankie, and now here he was, standing before them. They were very polite to my boyfriend. Very, very polite. Dad asked a zillion polite questions about his family and his summer and his interests, and Frankie told him with equal politeness what his parents did, and that he had a brother and a sister, and that most of his friends were away for the summer, and that he had started a garage band. (Mimi looked puzzled by this last piece of information.) Then Frankie said, "Speaking of interests, I hear that Claudia's a really good artist. I was wondering if I could see some of her paintings."

"Sure!" I exclaimed. I was extremely flattered. "Come on upstairs!"

I caught the horrified look on my parents' faces just in time. "I'll leave my door open," I hissed to my mother.

That didn't seem to be good enough. She got to her feet. For one awful second I thought she was going to say, "I'll come with you." Instead, she said, "I have a mountain of laundry to fold," and followed us up the stairs but detoured into her bedroom.

Frankie stepped into my room and looked around. "Whoa," he said. "Cool." He took in the easel, the shelves of brushes and paints and pastels and charcoals, the projects, both finished and unfinished, that covered most of the surfaces. "Claudia, you're amazing," he said after a few moments. "You're a really amazing artist." He leaned over to examine a study that I had done of my own left hand but didn't touch it. Now, how did Frankie know I didn't like people to touch my art?

"Thanks," I said.

"How does this . . ." Frankie paused, searching

117

for words, and started over. He gestured around the room. "How does this . . . come out of you?"

I shrugged and was pretty sure I began blushing. "I don't know. It's just . . . it's in me. And it comes out as art."

Frankie glanced toward the hallway, saw that my mother was nowhere in sight, and came to stand close to me, so close that I could feel his arm on my arm. And an incredible amount of heat.

I started talking then. I told Frankie about my art classes. I showed him the pieces in my portfolio. Frankie studied each one seriously and then murmured things like "You're so talented" or "That horse's hoof looks completely real."

I stood up and removed a sketch from my bulletin board. "Would you like to have this?" I asked. I handed him a drawing of a sparrow that sometimes sat on a tree limb outside my window.

"Really? I can have this?"

"Sure," I said. I imagined Frankie going home and pressing it between the pages of . . . well, I wasn't sure what Frankie liked to read, but I imagined him pressing it between the pages of something and keeping it for the rest of his life.

"Thanks!"

I sensed my mother hovering in the hall then and said to Frankie, "Want to go outside and watch for meteors?"

"Okay." We'd been sitting side by side on the

front stoop, watching for ten minutes (and not seeing a single meteor), when Frankie suddenly exclaimed, "Oh, no! I rode my bike over here and now it's dark. It's too late for me to ride home." He had to phone his parents then and ask one of them to come pick up him, which kind of put a damper on the evening, but that was okay. I knew I would lie in bed for a long time that night, remembering the warmth of his arm and the sound of his voice praising my drawings.

Mr. Evans was just loading Frankie's bicycle into the back of their station wagon when Janine's ride dropped her off. She stepped onto the sidewalk, arms loaded with books, and turned toward Frankie. He waved cheerfully to her, then climbed into the car.

I noticed that Janine did not return his wave, but I said, trying to sound as cheerful as Frankie had looked, "Want to watch for shooting stars?"

My sister stepped wordlessly onto the porch and disappeared through the front door.

There had been times in my life when I would have given anything for my annoyingly verbose (that means long-winded and wordy) sister to remain silent. But simple silence is way different, and far more pleasant, than the silent treatment. I wanted to yell something after Janine, but I knew she wouldn't have answered, which was why the silent treatment was the perfect form of torture.

* ★ *

The summer ground on. I began to feel like a character in a fairy tale—one of those fantasies in which the heroine disappears into another world where wonderful things happen and then returns to her own world to find out that no time has passed and nothing has changed. The hours I spent with Frankie were like the hours in the other world, all sweet and delicious and brand-new. And then Frankie would leave and I'd be stuck with Silent Janine and my disapproving parents and grandmother.

One afternoon I was standing before the easel in my bedroom, waiting for Frankie to call, and I remembered a day the previous summer when Kristy and Mary Anne and I had escaped a ferocious heat wave by going to the movies with Mimi. The four of us had sat in the back row of the theatre and laughed and laughed at the completely lame story of a dog and a cat who fought criminals (rats) in the New York City subway system. It was one of the stupidest movies I'd ever seen, but my friends and I couldn't stop laughing.

I put down my paintbrush now and thought, What do I care if Mary Anne plays with dolls? And does it really matter that Kristy would rather play Marco Polo than talk to boys?

I missed my friends. I should call them, I thought. I should ask them to go to the movies. Just the three of us, if Mary Anne's father would allow her to go into town without an adult.

I reached for my phone, and as I did so, it rang.

"Hello?" I said. (I almost said, "Hi, Frankie.")

"Hi, it's me. Mary Anne."

I swallowed my disappointment and managed to say, "That's so weird! I was just thinking about calling you."

"Really?"

"Yeah. But you go first."

"Okay. Well . . . I was wondering if you could come with me when I baby-sit for Jamie Newton next week. On Tuesday afternoon."

"Come with you?"

"Yeah. My dad has this rule." (Poor Mary Anne. Another rule.) "He lets me baby-sit now but not alone. Only with another sitter."

"Even in broad daylight?" I couldn't help asking.

I heard the pause at her end of the phone. "I know it's silly, but that's the rule."

"I'm sorry, Mary Anne. I didn't mean to be rude. But are we really talking about sitting just for Jamie for a couple of hours in the afternoon?"

"Yes. It will be a really easy job. . . . I'll give you most of the money."

"It's not that."

"Can't you come?"

I paused. "I can come. Tell Mrs. Newton we'll both be there."

"Okay."

The conversation felt unfinished.

"So, what were you going to call me about?" Mary Anne finally asked.

Oops. "What was I calling you about?" I thought frantically, the movie idea now seeming not so appealing. "I . . . was just calling to say hi."

Another long pause.

"Oh. Well, thank you for saying you'll come with me to the Newtons'."

"You're welcome." This was absolutely the worst phone conversation ever.

"Hey, Claud?"

"Yeah?"

"What's it like to have a boyfriend?"

I actually held the phone away from my face and stared at it. It wasn't *that* she had asked the question, it was the *way* she had asked it. If Dori had asked me the same thing she would have sounded all excited, as if she couldn't wait to have a boyfriend of her own and was gleefully gathering information for when that day came. But Mary Anne sounded all sort of plaintive and sorry for herself, like she was both worried she'd never have a boyfriend and afraid of what to do if she ever got one.

"Claudia?" said Mary Anne, and I realized I was still staring at the phone.

"Sorry."

"Was that a nosy question?"

I exhaled. "Not really. It's okay. I guess it's just a hard question to answer. I mean, because it's different for everyone."

"So you're saying Frankie really *is* your boyfriend?"

Now I heard something else in Mary Anne's tone, and I wouldn't have been surprised if she'd begun chanting "Claudia and Frankie, sitting in a tree. K-I-S-S-I-N-G!"

"You know what, Mary Anne? I'm not sure I can talk about this."

"Is it too painful?"

"Too painful?"

"You know, the pain of growing up."

This sounded like Mr. Spier talking, not Mary Anne. "What do you *really* want to know?" I finally asked. "Do you really want to know about Frankie and me, or is there something else?"

"I don't know."

"So . . ." I said.

"Um, okay. Well then, I'll see you next Tuesday at Jamie's. Two-thirty."

"Great. See you then."

I clicked off the phone and fell onto my bed.

★   ★   ★

In between then and two-thirty on Tuesday afternoon I had many talks with myself about being nice and patient with Mary Anne when we were at the Newtons' house. I reminded myself that Mary Anne had grown up without a mother and that there was nothing she could do about her father's strict rules. I tried to put the image of the mermaid bathing suit out of my head.

When Tuesday afternoon rolled around, I called good-bye to Mimi and walked to Jamie's house. I met Mary Anne as she was crossing the street.

"I know this is silly," she said. "I know it's silly to have two sitters for one kid, but . . ." She spread her hands as if to say, "What can I do about it?"

"That's okay. Anyway, Jamie's one of my favorite sitting charges."

Jamie Newton lived in our neighborhood, liked baby-sitters, and was cheerful, energetic, easygoing, and affectionate. Although lately his sunny attitude had clouded a bit. This was because he'd recently learned that in a few months he would become a big brother. His mother was going to have a baby in November. Jamie was trying to be grown-up about this, but it was plain to everyone that he preferred not to give up his status as the only child in the family.

I rang the doorbell and Mrs. Newton answered it with her finger to her lips. "Jamie went down for a nap a little while ago," she said quietly. "He'll probably sleep for about an hour."

I glanced at Mary Anne and saw that she was already blushing. "I'm sorry," she said. "I'm sorry that two of us have to be here, but . . ." Again she spread her hands.

"Not to worry. Jamie's thrilled that you'll both be here." Mrs. Newton reached for her purse. "All right. I won't be gone long. I'm just off to the doctor for a quick checkup. Here's my number," she went on, indicating a piece of paper on the kitchen table. "And Mr. Newton's number. Jamie can have a snack when he wakes up — there are chicken fingers in the fridge — and since it's a nice day, he'll probably want to play outside afterward, okay?"

Mary Anne and I nodded. Five minutes later, Mrs. Newton was gone and Mary Anne and I were sitting in the Newtons' living room, wondering what to do.

We didn't have to wonder for long.

"Hi-hi!" called a voice from the stairs.

"Jamie!" I said, grinning. "What are you doing up?"

"I couldn't sleep. Mommy said *two* sitters were going to be here, and that hasn't happened before, so I wanted to see."

Mary Anne and I smiled at each other.

"Here we are!" said Mary Anne brightly.

Jamie studied her intently. Finally, he said seriously, "I know you. You live across the street. Right?"

"That's right. My name is Mary Anne."

"Do I have to go back to bed or can I get up now?"

I glanced at Mary Anne. This was really her sitting job. I expected her to tell poor Jamie that he would have to stick to his mother's schedule, but to my surprise, she said, "I don't see any reason why you should lie around awake in your bed. Let's get a snack and then play outside."

"Goody!" cried Jamie. He made a dash for the kitchen, climbed on a stool, rummaged in a cupboard, and pulled out a box of chocolate-frosted cookies. "These are my favorites," he announced.

Mary Anne caught him as he slid off the stool, the box cradled in his arm. "Nice try," she said, gently slipping the box away from him and returning it to the cupboard. "I think these are a dessert item. Your mom said you could have chicken fingers." She peered into the refrigerator. "I'll bet you could also have an apple or a cheese stick."

"How about a doughnut?"

"How about an apple or a cheese stick?" said Mary Anne again, and I had to laugh.

Jamie finally accepted the cheese stick. He ate it slowly, and then the three of us went into the Newtons' backyard, which was equipped with a slide, a swing set, and a jungle gym. I carried the cordless phone outside with me in case Mrs. Newton called.

Jamie slid. He swung. He climbed. Mary Anne stood nearby and kept a careful eye on him. At last, Jamie said he was tired. "Do you want to go back inside?" Mary Anne asked.

Jamie nodded sleepily.

"I think maybe you should finish your nap," said Mary Anne, and she carried Jamie upstairs.

I sat on the Newtons' couch and wondered what to do with myself. When I heard Mary Anne singing to Jamie and realized it might be a while before she came back downstairs, I picked up the phone and dialed Frankie's number. I knew I shouldn't tie up a client's phone, but I was bored.

"Hi," I said when I heard Frankie on the other end of the line. Maybe it was my imagination, but his voice sounded as sweet and rich as a Hershey bar. "What are you doing?"

"Practicing. We're going to have a band rehearsal tonight. What are you doing?"

"Baby-sitting with Mary Anne. Remember the job I told you about? Mary Anne's upstairs putting Jamie down for a nap."

"Want to come to our rehearsal tonight? We'll be playing at Ryan's house."

"Sure! I just have to check with my parents."

"Cool," said Frankie. "So what else have you been doing today?"

I began to tell him about art class, and before I knew it, I heard Mary Anne's step on the stairs. I looked at my watch. Twenty minutes had passed. Twenty minutes that had felt like about twenty seconds, as opposed to the sadly endless conversation Mary Anne and I had had the week before. Why was it so easy to talk to Frankie and so . . . ? I left the question unasked.

Mary Anne had finished tiptoeing down the stairs by then. She was standing uncertainly at the bottom, looking into the living room, when she heard me say, "Hey, Frankie, I keep meaning to tell you . . ." Before I'd finished the sentence, she had slipped into the kitchen and closed the door silently between us.

1 1 stacey

Moving day was a day of lasts and firsts, all the last things coming at the beginning of the day, and the first things coming later.

Early that morning, I woke up in my room in our apartment for one last time. I was lying in bed, looking around at my blank walls and my nude windows, when my father knocked on the door and called, "Stace? The movers will be here in an hour."

I got dressed in a hurry. Not because I was afraid the movers would see me in my nightshirt, but because I couldn't wait to get out of New York City and on with my life. I rushed in and out of the bathroom and then down the hall to the kitchen, which had been packed up completely. There was not a speck of food in it. The drawers were empty, the cupboards were empty, the counters were bare. We had eaten dinner at Sal's the night before.

"Ready for one last meal at the Half Moon?"

asked my mother. The Half Moon was a diner at the end of our block.

"Definitely!" I exclaimed.

As we sat in a booth and waited for our eggs and toast and oatmeal, I said, "Do you think there are diners in Stoneybrook?"

"I'm not sure," said Dad, "but I imagine there's *a* diner, at least."

"There *are* restaurants, aren't there?" I asked, suddenly apprehensive.

"Of course," replied Mom. "We're moving to Connecticut, Stacey, not the prairie."

"Just checking."

We paid our last bill at the Half Moon, walked through its doors for the last time, and returned to our building.

"The movers are here," Tomas informed us as we approached the desk. "They got here about ten minutes ago. I let them upstairs."

"Thanks," said my parents.

We rode the elevator to our floor, where we found that the team of movers had already begun herding our furniture into the hall and lining it up by the entrance to the service elevator.

"I think it's time for us to get going," said Dad. "We'll just be in the way here."

So we gathered our purses and wallets and the few things we'd need on the drive to Connecticut in our new car. Mom and Dad spoke to the movers, and then we walked out of our apartment for the last time.

Last, last, last.

When we returned to the lobby, we were surprised to see a small crowd of people gathered around Tomas's desk. There were Twila and Jeremy and their parents, the Goldsmiths, and the Barkans. Twila ran to me, clasped my hands in hers, and wailed, "Don't go, Stacey! Don't go!"

Her mother gently unfastened our hands. "Twila, what did we just talk about?"

Twila scowled. "What I meant was, good luck and have fun."

I smiled. "Thanks."

With that, everyone began hugging.

"Come back and visit," said Mr. Barkan.

"You can stay in our apartment!" exclaimed Twila.

"Come visit us in Connecticut," said Mom, extending the invitation to the entire crowd.

"Anytime," added Dad.

A few minutes later we were settled in our car and Mom was steering it along the West Side Highway.

"Say good-bye to New York," Dad said to me over his shoulder.

Gladly. Good riddance to bad rubbish.

Bad rubbish = Laine.

"Bye, New York!" I said, and didn't even attempt to sound wistful.

We turned off the West Side Highway for one last time and crossed the George Washington Bridge for one last time. The city was behind me. Soon I could see nothing but trees and the interstate.

I fell asleep.

I dreamed I was at a slumber party at Laine's apartment, eating cupcakes and drinking lovely, sugary soda. It wasn't a very clever dream, and it made me feel sad, so that when I woke up, I was crabby.

"Where are we?" I asked groggily, rubbing my eyes and yawning.

"About half an hour from Stoneybrook," replied Mom.

Dad was now driving and Mom was sitting next to him, squinting at the directions from Manhattan to our new house.

"Another half an hour?" I whined. "This is endless."

My parents exchanged a glance. "Finish your nap," said Mom.

I sat in the backseat with my arms folded across my chest.

"The seat belt is too tight," I complained.

"Are you hungry?" asked my father, looking at me in the rearview mirror.

"No. I said the seat belt is too tight."

"And I asked if you're hungry."

I sighed. "Yes."

We pulled off the highway, found an enormous grocery store, much larger than any grocery store in the city, which surprised me, considering we were practically in the middle of nowhere, and Mom and I bought food for lunch while Dad stocked up on things to put in the cupboards and the refrigerator in our house.

We climbed back in the car and ate our lunch as we rode along, pine trees flying by outside the windows. (They were pretty much the only kind of tree I could identify.)

I was finishing my sandwich when I saw a green sign that read NEXT EXIT STONEYBROOK.

"We're almost there," said Mom.

My heart began to pound.

A minute later, Dad had turned off the highway and onto a smaller road. It was dotted with gas stations and car-parts stores. I saw a sign for a taxidermist. "Can we get a dog?" I asked.

"Maybe," said Mom.

"I don't know," said Dad.

I didn't really want a dog. I just wanted to see what my parents would say, now that we were in the country.

I was thinking that the road we were on wasn't terribly picturesque when Dad turned left and left again and then right, and finally I saw, for the first time, the sign that read WELCOME TO STONEYBROOK. The street we had turned onto was the opposite of the ugly one we'd been on just a few minutes before. It was as picturesque as a street in a book about picturesque New England towns.

"This is where we're going to live?" I couldn't help asking.

"This is it," replied Dad.

"Like it?" asked Mom.

I nodded. "Is this our street?" On either side of the road were trim houses with wide front lawns and gravel drives and trees, trees everywhere. Sweeping pines and reaching oaks (at least, I think they were oaks — they really could have been any kind of tree at all and I wouldn't have known the difference). It was a lovely, shady street. When I opened my window, I found that the air smelled good, a little like the air in the middle of Central Park.

"It's not our street," said Mom, "but it looks like ours. We thought we'd drive through town first."

Dad turned another corner and I got my first taste of downtown Stoneybrook. The street was much bigger than I had imagined any street in town would be. It was lined with shops and restaurants and businesses, and was crisscrossed by side streets, down which were more shops and restaurants and businesses. I saw a library and a doctor's office and a synagogue, a bank and a church and, yes, a diner.

"Hey, there's a department store!" I cried as we passed a brick building bearing the name BELLAIR'S.

"See? It's not so different from New York," said Mom.

"Except that I don't see buses or subway entrances or cabs—"

"There's a cab," said Dad.

"There's a bus," said Mom.

"Only one of each," I pointed out. But I was sitting up very straight, straining to look out the window and feeling happy about everything I saw. "I don't *want* this to be like New York. I want something different."

"We're all ready for a change," agreed my father.

Dad stayed on what I guessed was the main street in Stoneybrook until the stores and businesses came to an end and were replaced by small houses. Dad made another turn and then a few more, and at last he said, "Here it is. Fawcett Avenue."

The houses here were set closer to the road than the ones we had seen on our way into town, but they were just as tidy and Fawcett was just as shady. Almost everyone had a flower garden or two in the front yard, and I saw a few kids here and there and evidence of many more—bicycles and plastic riding toys and scooters and helmets.

"Which is our house?" I asked.

"Number six-twelve," Mom replied.

I watched the house numbers on the right side of the street climb slowly. "There it is," I said, and again I could feel my heart begin to pound. My first glimpse of our new home.

My father turned into the driveway of an empty-looking house. (Duh, of course it looked empty—it *was* empty.) I climbed out of the car and stretched my legs. I stepped onto our lawn. "It's weird to have grass right outside our door," I commented. "We don't even have to go to the park. It's kind of like we live in a park."

Mom and Dad smiled at me.

Our house was white with black shutters and a blue door. A winding brick path led from the driveway to the front stoop. I walked along it, feeling a little like Dorothy in *The Wizard of Oz*.

"Look at our front porch," I said, amazed.

"Don't forget the back porch," said Dad. "It's even bigger."

"Would you like to see your room?" asked Mom.

She unlocked the front door and I stepped into our house for the first time. The foyer was musty-smelling but clean. I walked through a living room, a dining room, a den, and a kitchen. I peeked into a little bathroom and stepped onto the back porch. "I can't believe there are more rooms upstairs!" I exclaimed. I felt as though I were in a palace.

I followed my parents to the second floor. "Here's your room," said Mom. "Picture it with curtains and a rug and of course all of your things."

I tried to. Then I walked to my window and looked outside. Trees, grass, a squirrel in a garden, a girl riding her bicycle along the sidewalk, a cat sitting on a driveway.

"What's that sound?" I asked.

"What sound?" said Dad.

"That. That weird buzzing-chirping-singing sound."

"I think it's a cricket," said Mom.

"I hope it's outside."

My parents and I walked through the house again and then explored our yard and walked up and down the street. Finally, Dad said, "Here come the movers."

We hurried back to our house to greet them.

★ ★ ★

We had an interesting afternoon. The movers unloaded their van and lugged our things inside. My parents ran around, saying, "That couch goes in here," or "Those boxes go upstairs."

137

A group of children gathered on the sidewalk in front of our house to watch the activity. Baby-sitting prospects, I thought. And then realized that there were probably other kids my age in the neighborhood who already sat for them. I wondered who they were and how long it would take to meet them.

Late in the day, just as the movers were loading their empty handcarts back into the van and I was standing with Mom and Dad in the mess that would someday be a tidy kitchen, our doorbell rang. My parents and I looked at one another. Who on earth could that be? The only people we knew in Stoneybrook were ourselves.

"Is it okay to answer the door?" I asked. In horror movies it was never a good idea.

My mother smiled. "I think so."

The three of us answered the door together and found a man and a woman and a little girl who looked about two.

"Welcome to the neighborhood!" said the woman. "I'm Stephanie Berk, and this is my husband, Tim, and our daughter, Lana."

The man held out a bakery box. "A little something for your first night in your new home."

"Thank you!" my parents and I said at the same time.

How interesting. People were as nice in the country as they were in the city.

We had more visitors that afternoon. My favorites were the Hansons, who supplied us with takeout menus.

"You can get takeout here?" I asked incredulously. I turned to Mom. "Let's get takeout tonight."

To my surprise, when we phoned the restaurant, we found out that it delivered.

"Just like in New York," I marveled.

When the food arrived, Mom and Dad and I carried it to our back porch and ate our first meal in our new home on our new lawn chairs.

"I feel like we're eating in the woods," I said, then paused. "Do you think there are any bears around here?"

My father coughed. "That's one worry you can cross off your list."

★   ★   ★

That night I climbed wearily into my old bed in my new room, ready for the first night in our new house. There were no curtains at the windows yet, and moonlight fell across the foot of the bed. I lay very still and listened. I had expected silence, but I found out that the country was noisy. I heard chirpings and rustlings and chitterings and buzzings (all coming from things that I desperately hoped were *not* in my room), and then I heard something that even I could recognize. It was the hoot of an owl. I recognized it because it sounded just like owls on television or in the movies: *Who, who-who, who-who. Who-who, who. Pause. Who, who-who, who-who. Who-who, who.*

I would hear that gentle *who-who*-ing on many, many more nights, and in time it would become as soothing and as familiar to me as car horns or the grinding gears of garbage trucks. It was my Stoneybrook lullaby.

12 KRISTY

One morning in July, when my birthday was still several weeks away, my mother and I had the following conversation:

Mom: Have you given any more thought to your birthday?

Me: You mean, do I want a party?

(Not long after Claudia's birthday, I had told Mom I didn't want to have a party of my own that summer.)

Mom nodded.

Me: No.

Mom: But you want some sort of family celebration, don't you?

Me: Yes, definitely.

Mom: Do you want to go out? What do you want to do?

Me: I want to have dinner at home. Just us. And Mary Anne. And maybe Claudia.

Mom: Nothing more than that? We could go to the beach for the day, or —

Me: No. Here is good.

If Dad was going to surprise me on my birthday, I wanted him to be able to find me. I didn't want the plans to be too complicated. Simpler was better where Dad was concerned.

Mom: Okay, so dinner here at home. On your actual birthday?

Me: Yup.

Mom: Great. I'll call Watson and make sure he's free. Maybe Karen and Andrew can come, too.

I don't know what kind of look crossed my face then, but whatever it was caused Mom's next words to come out more harshly than I think she had intended.

Mom: What? Watson isn't invited?

Well, no. I didn't want him at the party, especially not if Dad was going to show up.

Me (*very* uncomfortably): I just wanted, you know, a family party.

Mom: But you're inviting Mary Anne and Claudia.

Me: Yeah . . .

My mother turned away from me for a few moments. We were in the kitchen, sitting at the table together after a lazy Saturday breakfast, Louie patiently waiting for something to fall to the floor. Mom stood, gathered up our plates, and carried them to the sink. When she sat down again, she looked less strained.

Mom: It's your party, honey. You should do whatever you want . . . and invite whomever you want.

Mom was studying my face then, so I studied hers and got the unsettling feeling that there was something she wasn't saying. Did she know I had tried to write to Dad? I hadn't mentioned the letter to her, but maybe she'd seen it. After all, she was the one who had mailed the stack of envelopes that had been sitting on the hall table. Or maybe my father had called her and asked her something about my birthday.

Me (after a pause): Well, okay. Thanks. I'll talk to Mary Anne and Claudia and let you know if they can come.

As you can see, my birthday was a touchy subject.

It became an even touchier subject later on when I asked Claudia if she'd be able to come to dinner. I ran into her on the playground one afternoon while I was sitting for Claire and Margo, and she was sitting for Jamie Newton.

"Thanks, I'd love to come!" Claudia said, looking genuinely happy to have been invited. Then she added, "What night is your party?"

"The twentieth. It's a Friday."

Claudia's face fell. "Oh. I" (she made a big show of suddenly having to hold on to Jamie, even though he was riding on a kiddie swing and was strapped in tightly) "I can't. I'm busy that night. Frankie's family invited me to a barbecue and I already said I'd go. I'm really sorry."

"No problem," I replied, and hauled Claire and Margo off the jungle gym and walked them away, over their loud protests.

Claudia had seen Frankie about a thousand times since her birthday party. She had spent about five minutes with Mary Anne and me. And while it was true that I had absolutely no idea what was involved in having a boyfriend, it seemed to me that not alienating your existing girlfriends would be part of the deal. Claudia couldn't even come to my birthday dinner? I felt snubbed. I felt second best. But I wasn't going to say anything about it.

Loyal Mary Anne would be at the dinner, though. I'd invited her the very afternoon I'd spoken with Mom, and she had said she wouldn't miss it. "Miss one of your birthdays? I've never missed any of yours and you've never missed any of mine."

"You've been to more of my birthdays than my father has," I couldn't help remarking.

"That's weird, isn't it? . . . Kristy? Isn't it? . . . Yoo-hoo. Kristy."

"What? Oh, sorry."

"What were you thinking just now?"

I could feel myself begin to blush. "I know it's silly. In fact, it's totally ridiculous. But I was just hoping that maybe Dad would remember my birthday this year."

"Remember it how?"

"You know, send a card or a gift. Or . . . show up as a surprise."

"Kristy."

"I *said* it was totally ridiculous."

"All right. I hope you believe that."

"I do! I definitely, definitely do."

But I didn't really.

★　★　★

The summer had rolled along, with baby-sitting and swimming and softball and no word from my father. But I wasn't concerned. Well, not very. If he wanted to surprise me on my birthday, what better way to pull it off than to be completely out of touch beforehand?

Before I knew it, August 20th had arrived.

"Happy birthday! Happy birthday!" I was awakened by David Michael, who'd flung open my door (I didn't know whether he had knocked because I'd been soundly asleep) and jumped on my bed. "Happy birthday!" he cried again.

Soon Mom and Sam and Charlie were sitting on my bed with David Michael.

"One more year and you'll be a teenager," noted Charlie.

"Heaven help us. I'll have *three* teenagers," said Mom, but she was smiling.

"Girls make worse teenagers than boys do," commented Sam.

I punched him. "You made that up."

Sam grinned and shrugged.

"Come on downstairs," said Mom. "We have something special for you."

"Something special right now?" What could possibly happen at (I leaned over and peered at my alarm clock) 7:42? Could my father have arrived overnight?

Mom and my brothers cleared out of my room and I got dressed quickly. I stood at the top of the stairs. "Can I come down now?" I called.

From below I heard David Michael say, "Yes!" and then, "Make way for the Birthday Queen!"

I hurtled down the stairs and ran into the kitchen.

"Happy birthday!" said my family again.

I skidded to a stop. The table had been covered with a lime green cloth and set with blue and green paper plates, cups, and napkins. Glittery confetti in the shape of the number 12 and of teeny cakes and candles had been strewn along the center of the table, at one end of which were a little stack of cards and presents. Standing around the table were four people, the exact same people who had just been in my bedroom: Mom, Charlie, Sam, and David Michael. The table was set for five.

Okay. So Dad hadn't arrived overnight. But maybe one of those gifts . . .

"Here she is! The Birthday Queen!" David Michael announced, standing on tiptoe to place a paper crown with plastic jewels on my head.

I laughed. "Thanks!" I said. "I thought my party was tonight."

"It is," Mom replied. "But we thought we'd surprise you with a special breakfast. I called work and said I'd be a couple of hours late this morning. Come sit down."

So I sat. Mom carried plates of eggs and sausage and coffee cake to the table. She'd diced fruit, too, and we stuffed ourselves until Sam caught me eyeing the gifts. "Those are just decorations," he said.

"They are not!" exclaimed David Michael. "They're real. Open them, Kristy. Open them."

"Are they from you guys?" I asked.

Mom shook her head. "They're all things that came in the mail."

Aha! The mail. I wished I could have seen their outside wrappings to check for a return address from California, but Mom had thrown away the packages they'd arrived in.

I reached for the smallest present.

"That's from Aunt Colleen and Uncle Wallace," said Mom as I began to open the card that was taped to the box.

The card read "Happy Birthday to a Favorite Niece." Inside the box was an absolutely beautiful necklace that would look stunning on Claudia.

The next gift was from my aunt Theo and uncle Neal. It was a sixteen-month softball calendar.

My godmother had sent me a card that read "Nothing fancy, nothing funny, just a little spending money," in which she had enclosed a twenty-dollar bill.

There were other cards from other relatives, a bracelet from Watson, a baseball cap from my cousin Robin, a book from my grandmother, another book from my mother's college roommate.

"This is so much fun," I said at last, when I was stuffed with coffee cake and had piled my gifts and cards on the windowsill.

"Oh!" said my mother suddenly. "I just remembered. There's something else for you. Now, where did I put it?"

She left the kitchen and returned with a large envelope.

My hands began to tremble as I opened it.

"It's from everyone at work," said my mother cheerfully as I withdrew the oversize card that had indeed been signed by about thirty of Mom's coworkers.

I tried not to let my disappointment show. After all, there was still the party that evening.

Who knew what might happen then—or in the hours before then?

Later, after Mom had left for work, I carried my loot to my room. I was sorting through it when the doorbell rang and I heard Charlie yell, "Kristy! Claudia's here!" Then I heard feet pounding up the stairs, and there was Claudia.

"Happy birthday!" she cried. "I'm really sorry I can't come tonight."

"That's okay. I understand." But I didn't really.

Claudia thrust a present at me. "This is for you."

"Thanks!"

She had wrapped the box in pink-and-turquoise paper that I think she had made herself and tied it with sparkling silver ribbon. "This is so pretty," I said. I removed the paper carefully. Inside was a nail polish set.

"See?" said Claudia. "You can paint little decorations on your nails. That booklet shows you how. It includes designs for flowers and stars and hearts and rainbows. All sorts of things."

"Wow." Boy. "Wow. Thank you."

"You're welcome!"

When Claudia left, Sam poked his head in my room. "What's that?" he asked. He picked up the nail polish set. "Is this what Claudia gave you?"

I nodded.

He snorted. "Does she know you, or what?"

I laughed. But I was pleased that Claud had remembered my birthday. She'd made a card for me, too, and that pleased me even more. I imagined her across the street, sitting at her desk, surrounded by her markers and papers and fancy scissors and punches, creating a card and wrapping paper just for her old friend.

The afternoon of my birthday passed v-e-r-r-r-y slowly. When I saw the mail truck from my window, I dashed outside and waited by our box for Nancy, our letter carrier. As I had hoped, there were more birthday cards among the bills and catalogs she handed me. Three more, in fact.

One from the Pikes, signed by all the kids.

One from the Newtons.

One from the Goldmans.

I added them to my stash and told myself that the best was yet to come.

Exactly how slowly could a day go by? I arranged my cards on the desk in my room. I started writing my thank-you notes. I watched as Frankie's mother pulled up at the Kishis' to take Claudia to the Evans family barbecue. At long last, Mom's car turned into our driveway. I pressed my nose to the screen in an effort to see whether my mother was the only person in the car.

She was.

She climbed out, carrying a large cake-size box.

I met her downstairs.

"Party time!" said Mom.

Mary Anne arrived a few moments later, and before I knew it, she and Sam and David Michael and I were sitting on the back porch, laughing and talking, while Mom and Charlie started the grill, Louie sitting at strict attention at Charlie's feet in case a whole hamburger should suddenly fall to the ground.

The phone rang and I answered it in a hurry.

"Happy birthday!" said a deep voice. "So, how does it feel to be twelve years old?"

"Watson?" My heart, which had been beating fast, slowed to an annoyed crawl. "Well, you know . . ." I tried to think how to answer that stupid question and finally said, "Thank you for the bracelet. I really like it. It was very thoughtful of you."

I hung up the phone, and while we were waiting for the burgers to cook, Sam said, "So, everyone, what was your most memorable birthday?"

"The time Mom dropped my cake," said David Michael promptly.

"The year we were in Florida on my birthday and we went to a spring training game," said Charlie.

"The year my dad hired a magician to come to my party," said Mary Anne.

I was half listening to the conversation. The other half of me was calculating time (in other words, what time Dad might show up if he had left California in the morning) and trying to figure out if any of the presents Mom had brought outside were from someone other than the people on the patio.

"Kristy?" said Sam. "What was your most memorable birthday?"

I shook myself. "Oh," I said. I usually found it hard to answer a question like that, but suddenly I had an answer. "My fifth birthday. Remember? That was the year when no one could come to my party. We'd invited Mary Anne and Claudia, of course, and a bunch of kids from my preschool class. And not one single person could come. Everyone was either away on vacation or busy. And I'd been just desperate for a real party — one with games and goody bags and everything. Plus, Dad had said he knew this farm that could provide you with a pony for two hours, so all the party guests could go on rides around the backyard. But one after another, the parents phoned and said their kids wouldn't be able to come. I remember crying when the last parent said no.

"But Dad told me not to be sad. He said something special was going to happen anyway, and sure enough, at lunchtime on my birthday, I found a note on my plate. I couldn't read it, but you and Dad helped me," I said to Mom.

"I remember that!" Sam exclaimed suddenly. "The note was a clue. The first clue in a birthday scavenger hunt."

I nodded. "Dad had made a clue for each of my presents. The last clue led me into the backyard, and that was where I found the pony. Not to keep, of course. But a pony to ride, just like I had wanted. So I had a party with you guys" (I nodded to Charlie and Sam) "and a pony. It wasn't exactly the party I had imagined, but when I saw that pony standing under the tree," (my gaze shifted to an elm tree, under which, seven years ago, a brown-and-white pony had stood, stamping its feet impatiently) "I thought Dad was . . ." I wasn't sure how to finish the sentence. I was going to say that I'd thought he was magic, but I didn't want to hurt Mom's feelings.

Luckily, David Michael interrupted to ask, rather indignantly, "Where was *I*?"

"You weren't born yet," Sam told him.

"Oh," said David Michael.

Everyone looked at me again. I looked back at the elm tree.

Mom cleared her throat.

Charlie checked on the grill.

"Well," said Mary Anne.

When the food was ready, we ate at the picnic table. Afterward, Mom waited until darkness was falling before she served the cake, and that was why I saw the first meteor of the evening just as I blew out the candles. That must be a good sign, I said to myself. What could be better than making a birthday wish, blowing out candles, and seeing a shooting star all at the same time?

I tackled my gifts with renewed hope—and an eye on the back door.

My gifts were lovely. David Michael had made me a lanyard at his elementary school playground program.

"You can use it for a key chain," he told me proudly.

Sam had bought me a copy of the *Guinness Book of World Records*, Charlie had gotten me a new softball, Mary Anne had had a special jersey made up for me (I almost cried when I opened it, but I am not really a crying sort of person), and my mother gave me a watch.

"Mom!" I exclaimed. "This is—"

I was about to say that it was too expensive and that we couldn't afford such things, but she waved her hand and said, "I wanted my special daughter to have a special present."

I started to reach for the next gift when I realized that there weren't any more. I had opened them all. I looked over my shoulder. Surely Dad would stride in now, right now. It would be the most dramatic moment for his arrival. But Mom got to her feet, yawned, and said, "We'd better get cleaned up." My brothers began to help her.

I looked at the back door again, and then at Mary Anne. I didn't have to say anything to her. She sat down next to me on the bench and put her arm across my shoulders.

That was how my birthday ended.

1️⃣3️⃣ MARY ANNE

"I thought these stupid meteors were going to bring us good luck," said Kristy sullenly as we sat on her patio with the remains of her birthday dinner scattered around us.

"You did? Really?" I replied.

"Well, I don't know. I guess I didn't. But I thought maybe they could bring . . . something."

"You mean your father."

Kristy shrugged.

"You really thought your father was going to come, didn't you?" I pressed.

"I didn't know if he'd come, but I wanted him to. I hoped he would."

I reached out and plucked a candle from the edge of her cake. I licked the frosting off of the end and said, "You know, every year I wish my mother could somehow spend my birthday with me. When I was little, I used to pretend she was right there but invisible, watching me open presents and play games and take the first bite of cake. Now I just wish I could have a conversation with her. You know, tell her what's been happening and how school's been going. Nothing earth-shattering. Just . . . stuff."

"I try to do that with Dad. That's what I tell him about in my letters. Just stuff. But he didn't even get the last letter."

"It's weird," I said. "We take something as nice as a birthday and we ruin it by wishing for something impossible."

"Dad *could* have come," Kristy said fiercely. "It wasn't impossible." Then she softened. "When I picture my father, I picture him as he was the last time I saw him. How do you picture your mother?"

"The way she looks in that photo in Dad's bedroom," I replied. "Their wedding photo. So when I imagine her at my birthday parties, she's always in her white gown with the veil and the flowers."

Kristy smiled. Finally, she said, "Well, I have my mom and my brothers, and you have your dad."

"And we have each other," I added.

"Yup," said Kristy.

Later, when I was getting ready for bed, I looked out my window. I checked Kristy's window across the way to see whether she was still awake. She wasn't. At least, her light wasn't on.

I turned my eyes to the sky, but I didn't see any more shooting stars, so I slid under the covers and thought about the next day, which would be Kristy Day. As bad as I felt for my friend, I couldn't help also feeling excited about the event I had planned—although I was disappointed that Claudia wasn't going to be part of it.

A few days earlier, not long after the embarrassing afternoon at Jamie Newton's, I had seen Claudia sitting alone on her front stoop, so I had joined her. "Are you waiting for Frankie?" I had asked, first thing.

"I'm not *always* waiting for him," she'd replied in a tone of voice that indicated extreme irritation.

For heaven's sake. It wasn't as if I had already asked her this question a billion times. I'd considered saying something equally rude back to her, but I'd wanted to invite her to Kristy Day, and figured it was better not to get off on the wrong foot with the conversation.

I'd shrugged my shoulders. Then I'd said, "So, next week is Kristy's birthday."

"I know. I'm really sorry I can't come to her supper."

I'd nodded. "But I'm planning something for the next day. Something special just for Kristy, called Kristy Day."

Claudia had smiled. "Very original."

I'd smiled, too, and tried to figure out how to explain the event without mentioning Kristy's secret hope that her father would remember her birthday. In the end, I'd sort of skirted the issue by saying simply that since Kristy wasn't going to have a party this year I'd thought we should plan some kind of surprise for her.

"And since you can't come to her supper, maybe you could come to Kristy Day. I know that would make her happy."

Claudia had brightened. "Really? You want me to come?"

"Of course."

"When did you say Kristy Day is? The day after her birthday?"

I'd nodded.

And Claudia's face had fallen.

"I'm going to the beach with Frankie and his family that day," she'd said. "If I'd known about Kristy Day, I never would have said yes."

Huh. So what, exactly, had been so annoying when I'd asked earlier if she was waiting for Frankie? It had seemed like an entirely reasonable, sane question, since apparently she was *always* doing something with Frankie or waiting to do something with him. Or with his family.

I didn't lose my temper very often, but when I did . . . watch out. I'd thought about the injustices of this particular conversation and I could feel my temper bubbling to the surface. I'd been about to say, "So enlighten me. *Why* were you insulted just now when I asked if you were waiting for Frankie?" But then I'd turned and caught the look on Claudia's face, and I'd closed my mouth.

"I'm really sorry," Claud had said. And she'd certainly looked very, very sorry. Which had been nice but also sort of confusing. I'd thought she wanted to spend every waking moment with her boyfriend. But apparently not. Maybe this summer, this summer during which Claudia seemed to be shooting away from Kristy and me, was as hard on her as it was on us.

Maybe she missed us.

"That's okay." I'd thought for a moment. "Hey! We could hold Kristy Day some other time." But then I'd shaken my head. I'd had a feeling Kristy would need her day as soon as possible after her birthday, that she would need immediate cheering up.

"No. Don't switch things around for me," Claud had said.

And so I hadn't.

Now it was the night before Kristy Day, and Kristy did indeed need her big day. I willed myself to sleep.

★   ★   ★

When I woke in the morning, it was to sunshine and a sky as clear and blue as a lagoon (not that I'd ever seen a lagoon). I leaped out of bed, ate breakfast in a hurry, and phoned Mrs. Pike to make sure it was still okay for me to borrow her house and yard and kids.

"Come on over," she said.

I walked to the Pikes' house, carrying two grocery bags. They were packed with construction paper, crayons, markers, empty egg cartons, a box of macaroni, glue, glitter, pipe cleaners, a package of Popsicle sticks, empty soup cans, and a roll of butcher paper. I had been saving the soup cans and the egg cartons since I'd gotten the idea for Kristy Day. I had bought the rest of the things with the last of my money. (I needed some more sitting jobs.)

The fastest route to the Pikes' took me directly past Kristy's house, and I sincerely hoped she wouldn't catch sight of me and my overloaded possessions. I stared straight ahead, struggling with the bags, as if, by not looking at the Thomases' house, Kristy couldn't spot me.

When I finally turned onto Slate Street, the Pike kids, all eight of them, were waiting for me in their driveway.

"Hi, Mary Anne!" they called.

"We're ready for Kristy Day!" added Vanessa.

"Whatever that is," said Nicky.

"Didn't your parents explain it to you?" I asked. I'd had a long conversation with Mr. and Mrs. Pike.

"Maybe. I don't remember."

The kids followed me into their backyard, where I set the bags on the patio.

"Kristy needs some cheering up," I began. "And—"

"Why?" interrupted Margo. "Why does she need cheering up?"

Mallory nudged her sister. "That's none of our business," she whispered loudly.

Margo looked unconvinced, so I said, "You know how sometimes you have a bad day? Well, Kristy has had a lot of bad days this summer, and I thought she would feel better if we made a special *good* day for her. Kristy Day. We can tell her how much we like her, and we can make her some presents. We're even going to have a parade for her."

"A parade?" exclaimed Claire. "Are we going to be in it?"

"Of course we are, dummy," said Adam. "*We're* the parade."

"Will there be elephants?" asked Claire.

"Excuse me?" I said.

"Will there be elephants? In the parade?"

The triplets turned red with unexploded laughter, and Mallory glared at them.

"Well, no," I replied. "It will just be us in the parade. I mean, just people. We're going to carry banners—we have to make them first—and then we'll march down your street and over to

Bradford Court and right by Kristy's house. Other people will join the parade on the way. Oh, and in a little while, Jenny Prezzioso's father is going to bring her over here. She's going to help us with the presents and the banners."

"Will everyone see us marching in the parade?" cried Vanessa. "Oh, I hope so. I hope everyone sees us!"

"What kind of presents are we going to make for Kristy?" asked Byron.

I began to unload the supplies. The kids crowded around the picnic table to watch. "We can make caterpillars out of egg cartons," I began.

Jordan's mouth dropped open. "I did that in preschool!" he exclaimed, affronted.

"Hey! *I'm* in preschool!" cried Claire.

"Then that will be the perfect project for you," I said hastily. "And for Jenny. We can also make pencil holders out of soup cans—"

"How many pencil holders does Kristy need?" asked Adam.

"Adam," said Mallory warningly.

"Okay, okay."

"You can make jewelry with the macaroni," I continued, but I could feel my cheeks burning, "and all sorts of things with the Popsicle sticks. You could also make cards for Kristy. And of course we need to work on the banners. We need one banner for the front of the parade that will say 'Kristy Day,' and another for the back of the parade that will say 'We Love You, Kristy!'"

Nicky pretended to choke. "Does it have to say 'love'?"

"Yes," I said firmly. "Now, let's get to work."

Despite various unhelpful comments from Nicky and the triplets, the Pike kids did in fact get to work, and soon Kristy's gifts were piling up. Jenny Prezzioso arrived and she got to work, too. Jenny, who was three years old and friends with Claire, lived not far from the Pikes. She adored Kristy, and I had thought she would be a good addition to the parade, but the instant she arrived I sensed trouble. For one thing, she was the youngest kid at the Pikes' and she needed a lot of help with everything. For another, she was wearing a white sundress, frilly white socks, and white patent leather party shoes, even though her parents knew it was a morning of arts and crafts.

I put Mallory in sole charge of Jenny, and the first thing Mallory did was find a smock for her to wear.

I felt that the morning had gotten off to a shaky start, but by eleven-thirty we had not only a nice pile of presents for Kristy but two brilliantly colored banners. Lauren Hoffman and the Shillaber twins showed up at the Pikes' as planned, so they could walk in the parade. Unfortunately, no one noticed until we were halfway down Slate Street

164

that the banner for the back of the parade read
WE LOVE YOU, KISTY, but by then there was nothing
we could do about it.

We continued down Slate Street, attracting
a certain amount of attention. Kids who were
out riding their bikes and playing in their yards
stopped to watch us. Cars slowed down as we
went by, and a couple of the drivers honked their
horns cheerfully. Vanessa, who was holding one
side of the front banner, walked regally, turning
from one side of the street to the other, a gracious
smile on her face, as if she were a beauty queen.
Claire and Margo grinned and waved, held their
presents aloft, and cried, "Happy Kristy Day!" as
they ran along.

A few minutes later we turned onto Bradford
Court. Standing on the corner were Mrs. Newton,
Jamie, and David Michael. I had phoned Mrs.
Newton just before we left the Pikes' house so she
could have the boys ready.

"Is Kristy at home?" I asked David Michael
nervously as he joined the parade. It had only now
occurred to me that Kristy might have left the
house and wouldn't be at home as her personal
parade passed by. But David Michael nodded,
and I let out a sigh of relief before I said, "Okay,
everyone—now!"

We slowed the parade down and began
chanting, "Kris-*ty*! Kris-*ty*!" until she stepped

cautiously onto the Thomases' front stoop and stood there motionless. It was one of the few times in Kristy's life when she was at a loss for words.

I grinned. Just like on Slate Street, kids who were outside playing had put down their toys to stare at our parade. Faces appeared in windows and people stepped out of doorways. I saw Mimi, Janine, the Goldmans, Mrs. Thomas, and my dad. And I noticed a girl I had never seen before—a girl about my age, with blonde hair and blue eyes, straddling a brand-new bicycle. She looked puzzled, but she was smiling. And she stopped to watch as Kristy slowly crossed her yard.

"Happy Kristy Day!" I cried as my best friend neared the sidewalk.

I led the parade past her and then we turned around. The turning-around was accomplished clumsily, and by the time we were standing in front of Kristy again, both banners were facing backward and Claire and Jenny had dropped their presents.

"The banners, the banners!" I hissed, and the kids sorted themselves out. (I thought I heard Nicky mutter "We love you, Kisty," but I wasn't sure.)

After that, the parade fell apart, but this was okay. The kids showered Kristy with their gifts, and Claire and Jenny declared loudly that Kristy was their favorite baby-sitter.

Later, when our friends had gone home and Kristy and I had returned the last little kid to his parents, we walked back to Bradford Court. "Remember last night?" asked Kristy. "When I said that I have my mom and my brothers and you? I should have added that I have my friends, and all the kids I sit for, and our neighbors, too."

"I know that doesn't exactly make up for your father, but it's something, isn't it?" I said.

"It's definitely something. I'm lucky and I know it."

"And *I'm* lucky and *I* know it. I have your mom and your brothers and Claudia and Mimi. And you."

"We get what we get," said Kristy. "And you and I have a lot. I'm going to hang the parade banners in my room."

"We love you, Kisty," I said, and she grinned.

★　★　★

"And you'd been planning Kristy Day for how long?" my father asked me later that afternoon.

I shrugged. "A couple of weeks."

"I think it meant a lot to her."

I nodded, again unable to explain why she needed a special day so badly.

Dad patted the couch and I sat down next to him. "I've seen a big change in you this summer,

Mary Anne. I'm proud of you. You've done a lot of growing up."

"Thanks," I said.

"I think," he went on, "that you're ready to baby-sit alone."

"Yes!" I cried.

"In certain situations."

"Okay."

"And with a curfew."

"Okay."

I didn't care. As long as we were moving forward.

After dinner I sat in my room—my pink room with the *Alice in Wonderland* and Humpty Dumpty pictures—and I considered sorting through the box of my mother's things again. I got as far as opening it and removing a journal my mother had kept when she was in college. But I had already read the journal. And I was now familiar with every other item in the box. I didn't need to touch and study and hold on to the pieces of my mother's life anymore.

I slid the box under my bed. It was enough to know it was nearby.

1 4 CLAUDIA

I slathered SPF 30 lotion on my arms and legs and face while I waited, once again, for Frankie to arrive. Yesterday the beach, today swimming at the community center. Thanks to Frankie, it had been a very outdoors-in-the-sun kind of summer (especially after his statistics class had ended), and I wasn't taking any chances with my skin.

The beach had been fun, although I'd sort of had this feeling that Frankie had been hoping the day would hold more than just sitting under the umbrella with his family and me. He hadn't talked to me as much as usual, and he'd kept looking up and down the beach. For what?

I'd actually said, "What are you looking for?" And he'd given me an embarrassed smile and replied, "Oh, you know."

I did not know. I hadn't known at the beach, and I still didn't know now as I waited for him to come pedaling along Bradford Court on his bicycle. Maybe he'd just been bored. There hadn't been a lot to do at the beach. There was no boardwalk and not even a snack bar. I'd been all for riding the waves, but Frankie hadn't seemed interested. Maybe he hadn't wanted to hang out with his family again.

If that had been the case, then today promised to be better. Frankie and I would be on our own.

I spotted Frankie turning the corner onto Bradford. I checked my watch. He was only twenty minutes late. Well, twenty-two, to be exact. I looked again. And now twenty-two minutes and four seconds.

I stood up and waved.

"Ready?" Frankie called. He didn't bother to get off his bicycle. In fact, he didn't even turn up my driveway, just waited on the street, straddling the bike. I have to say he looked a little impatient. I considered pointing out that he was the one who was late and I was the one who had had to wait, but thought better of it.

We rode through town to the community center, where there were three excellent outdoor pools: an actual Olympic-size pool, a wading pool, and a diving pool. The Olympic pool was where most people hung out, and the high school kids had long made a particular corner of it their own. It was one of the corners at the deep end and was shaded by a maple tree, which was good for those who wanted to stay out of the sun. The tree was bordered by a large grassy area, and as

Frankie and I approached, I could see that quite a few kids had already spread their towels in the sunshine. Some were soaking up the rays, others were sitting and talking, listening to music, eating hot dogs and chips from the snack bar.

I didn't know any of the kids, though, so I headed for the tree and spread my towel under it.

Frankie stared at me. "What are you doing?"

"I—What do you mean, what am I doing?"

"We'll look like outcasts by ourselves over here. I want to sit with my friends."

Well, if he wanted to sit with his friends he should have told me they were his friends in the first place. I wasn't a mind reader. His friends had been away at camp and on vacation all summer. This was the first time I'd met any of them.

I shrugged and followed Frankie into the crowd of kids.

Our arrival was heralded by a chorus of greetings. And by "our" arrival, I mean Frankie's. Apparently, something had happened to me that morning and I had been rendered invisible.

"Frankie!"

"Hi, Frankie!"

"Frankie, I missed you when I was at camp!"

I feel I must point out here that while a number of boys were in this crowd, all the greetings flowed from the mouths of girls. And the moment

Frankie spread his towel on the grass, no fewer than five of those girls edged their towels closer to his.

Luckily, I saw what was happening, and I spread my towel next to Frankie's, jumped on it, and lay down flat, claiming the space for myself before any of the intruder girls could do the same. It barely mattered. The girls just rearranged themselves so that they were as close to Frankie's other side as was scientifically possible.

I glared fiercely at them, but since they had glommed their eyes onto Frankie, they didn't even see me. Anyway, there was the invisibility issue.

"So what have you been doing all summer, Frankie?" asked this one girl with gleaming black hair and shining flawless skin the color of chestnuts.

Frankie gave her a charming grin. "Nothing much. You know, hanging."

Excuse me? I was "nothing much"?

I sat up on one elbow, leaned over to Frankie, and cleared my throat.

He glanced at me, but before he could say anything, another girl, this one with rippling brown hair and skin so pale she must ordinarily have staked out territory under the maple tree, moved over until she was sitting half on her towel and half on Frankie's. "My sister said Stoneybrook

High has been waiting years for someone as cute as you to arrive."

My mouth dropped open. First of all, who said things like that? And second of all . . . well, I couldn't think of a second of all. The first of all was bad enough.

Frankie gave the girl a lazy smile.

"Can you believe that in two and a half weeks we'll be in high school?" asked a third girl.

I sat all the way up and cleared my throat louder than before.

"Oh!" exclaimed the girl with the black hair, and suddenly the others seemed to see me.

"Who's this?" asked one.

"Is she your sister?" asked another.

"Nope. This is Claudia Kishi," said Frankie, and he might as well have been giving a tour of his house and suddenly got to the boring part—a closet. That was the amount of enthusiasm he was able to muster when he said my name. "Claudia, these are my friends Anna" (she was the girl with the flowing brown hair), "Lindy" (she was the girl who wanted to know what Frankie had been doing all summer), "Tracy" (she was the one who was excited about starting school), "Alexa, Morgan, and Val." (Blah, blah, and blah.)

"So," said Tracy, "which middle school did you go to?"

"Stoneybrook," I replied. "SMS."

"Really? I don't remember seeing you in any of my classes."

I cleared my throat for the third time. "I'll be in seventh grade this year."

Six pairs of eyes turned themselves on Frankie. I waited for him to say something like "Claudia is a really good artist" or "Claudia and I had so much fun at the beach yesterday" (although that would not, in fact, be true). But he didn't, and the girls seemed to lose interest in me. I couldn't blame them.

"You know what Lindy did this summer?" Anna said to Frankie. "She went to *Spain* with her family. For six weeks."

"Wow," said Frankie.

"Hey, did you guys hear that new Cloudy Dan song?" asked Alexa.

"Yup," said Frankie.

Of course he had.

Minutes later, one of the girls seemed to remember my presence. I think it was Morgan. "What did you do this summer, Claudia? Go to day camp?"

Huge peals of laughter. Hee-hee. Ha-ha. I tried to join in, but Frankie was laughing, too, and besides, something had happened to my vocal cords. I couldn't get them to work.

174

"Frankie, are you going to try out for the football team?" Lindy wanted to know.

Frankie shrugged as if this hadn't occurred to him, but I could tell he was pleased that a cute girl thought he was football-team material.

"I hope I get nominated for Homecoming Queen," said Val.

"Homecoming Queen! You can't be Homecoming Queen when you're a freshman!" exclaimed Anna.

"No, but I can start getting noticed, so that in a couple of years everyone at SHS will know who I am."

"Frankie, want to go in the water?" asked Alexa.

"Sure!" he said, and jumped to his feet.

Morgan glanced down at me. "Have you passed your swimming test?" she asked, all innocently.

I scowled at her. "*Yes.*"

★   ★   ★

Somehow I survived the rest of the day. Frankie didn't *totally* ignore me. At one point he asked me (just me, not the rest of his harem) if I wanted to go swimming, which I did. Later he asked me if I wanted ice cream, which I didn't because I had lost my appetite.

Finally, when people began to pack up their floats and towels and sunscreen and kids, Frankie and I made our way back to our bicycles. "Well," said Frankie as he fiddled with the lock. "That went . . ." He didn't finish the sentence. He didn't have to.

So he'd noticed. Although it would have been hard not to notice.

"Yeah," I said. "What happened?"

"*You* know," said Frankie.

Once again, I did *not* know. And apparently Frankie wasn't going to enlighten me. We rode along in silence. When we reached my driveway, I slowed to a stop. "See you—" I started to say, hand extended in a wave. But Frankie was already riding off.

I didn't hear from him for several days after that. At first, I was so humiliated that I didn't care. At least that's what I told myself. But as two days turned into three and then four and five, I began to wish he would call. I could have called him, of course, but I wanted him to call me. I wanted him to see the error of his ways and apologize. I wanted a phone call like someone would get on a soap opera. "Claudia, can you ever forgive me? I can't believe how insensitive I was. My friends were so rude. I don't know what I was thinking. Let's go to the movies tonight, okay? I'll make it up to you."

Needless to say, that didn't happen. On the sixth day, just when I couldn't stand it any longer and was about to give in and call him, my phone rang. And it was Frankie!

"Hi!" I exclaimed. I was ready to forgive and forget.

"Claudia, I have to tell you something."

I hesitated. "Okay. Do you want to come over?"

"No, I can say it on the phone."

"Oh."

"All right," said Frankie. "It's this: I don't think we should see each other anymore."

"What? *Why?* What do you mean?" I could almost hear him shrugging on the other end of the phone. When he said nothing, I pressed on. "Frankie, you have to tell me why you're, um, breaking up with me."

"Well, you know, I'll be in high school this year." (Duh.) "The kids are older." (Duh.) "And it was a really fun summer, but . . ." He trailed off.

I knew what he wasn't saying. It had been a fun summer, but Frankie didn't want to enter SHS as the freshman with the seventh-grade girlfriend. Especially not with Morgan and Val and the rest of the girls hovering around him like Tinker Bell around Peter Pan. Still . . .

"But why does that mean we can't see each other? Can't we still go to the mov—"

"Claudia, it's over," said Frankie, and he hung up.

For a few moments I just stared at the phone in my hand. Then I hung up, too.

I had been dumped.

Tears came to my eyes in an instant, and I lay on my bed and sobbed. I didn't even consider calling Frankie back. I had heard the finality (and the exasperation) in his voice. I cried until my hair was damp from tears. At last I reached for my phone again. I started to dial Kristy's number, then hung up. I started to dial Mary Anne's number, then hung up. They wouldn't understand. Or maybe they would understand, but they wouldn't know what to say. I could call Dori, but her family was away on vacation. Ditto Emily and her family.

At last I stumbled to my feet and made my way downstairs. Mimi was making tea in the kitchen. The moment she saw me she put her arms around me. "My Claudia! You have been crying. Tell me what is the matter."

I allowed myself to be enveloped in Mimi's arms for a while. At last I said with a sob, "Frankie dumped me."

"My poor Claudia. Come. Sit down. Have a cup of tea with me."

I sat. Mimi poured the tea.

"I don't know what I did wrong," I wailed.

"My Claudia, I am sure you did nothing wrong."

"Then why doesn't he want to be with me?"

"It is difficult sometimes when friends are of different ages. Frankie is about to enter a new phase in his life. Can you see how it might be hard to remain his . . . his girlfriend when you'll be in middle school and he'll be starting high school? He'll have a lot to get used to—"

"Like high school girls," I muttered.

"That will be part of it," agreed Mimi. "He'll also have more schoolwork, and different activities, and he'll be meeting new friends. But you'll be making new friends this year, too. And that's what you and Frankie *should* be doing. Branching out and making new friends. You are a bit young for a relationship that lasts a long time. You also have your old friends." Mimi looked solemnly at me.

"Kristy and Mary Anne?" I said.

She nodded.

"They seem so much younger than me."

"Friends grow up at different rates. That can be difficult, too. But Kristy and Mary Anne will catch up to you. I know you've been hurt by the distance you feel from them, and I think they feel hurt as well. I also think your friendship can change if the three of you work on it."

"Okay," I said uncertainly.

Mimi poured herself another cup of tea. "My Claudia, there's someone I think you need to talk to."

"Someone besides Mary Anne and Kristy?"

"Yes."

I lowered my eyes. "Is it Janine?"

"Yes," said Mimi again. "Things have not been right between you and your sister since your birthday, and it is time to change that. Do you think you can take the first step and talk to her? Tonight?"

I let an enormous sigh escape. "Okay."

★　★　★

I waited until dinner was over and Janine was in her room, seated before her computer. Then I knocked on her door. "Can I come in?"

Janine looked at me in surprise but said, "All right."

"So . . . Frankie dumped me today," I told her, first thing. I was leaning against the doorjamb with my arms folded across my chest.

Janine raised her eyebrows and turned off the computer.

"Which means he's available," I continued. "But good luck fighting your way through Val and Anna and Lindy and Tracy."

Janine waved her hand. "Oh, them," she said, as if they were houseflies.

"Do you even know them?"

"Not very well. But I know their kind."

I smiled.

Janine patted her bed, and I sat on the edge. She sat next to me.

180

"I'm really sorry about everything," I told her. "I didn't know you liked Frankie. I mean, not at first. And I was surprised when it turned out that he liked me. But, well, he was a high school guy, almost, and, I don't know. It was just really flattering. I felt grown-up. And Mary Anne and Kristy seemed like such babies. And—"

"That's okay, Claudia," said Janine. "You don't have to say any more. I was hurt, and you didn't seem to care. But I knew there was no chance for Frankie and me. And that's what I was really mad about."

I gave my sister a hug. But when I fell into bed that night I felt lonely. No Frankie. Nothing had changed with Mary Anne and Kristy. And I still felt like I was the great big sore thumb of my family.

I looked out my window. Bradford Court was dark and quiet. I waited until I saw a shooting star before I slipped under the covers and fell asleep.

1 5 KRISTY

"I have an idea," I said.

"Yeah? What?" Claudia sounded interested.

"You're baby-sitting for Jenny Prezzioso this afternoon, right?"

"Right."

"Well, I'm sitting for David Michael, and Mary Anne is sitting for Jamie. Let's take the kids to the school playground. That way you and Mary Anne and I can hang out. Okay?"

"Okay. I mean, great! That's a great idea, Kristy."

"Meet you at the playground at two?"

"Excellent. See you later."

I hung up the phone. This was not a bad way to spend the last day of summer vacation. Claud had even seemed excited about it. Which meant that she actually *wanted* to hang out with Mary Anne and me—following a summer in which just the opposite had seemed to be true. In fact, it had finally begun to feel that Claud wasn't even our friend anymore; that her friendship with us had fallen away like old socks slipping out of a laundry basket. It was a positive sign that she wanted to see Mary Anne, me, and three very young children instead of making plans to see Frankie Evans, or painting alone in her room like a tortured female Van Gogh, or running downtown to buy her thirty-eighth pair of extra-cool shoes. It was, I hoped, the first step in rebuilding an important and old friendship. I would have allowed the friendship to slip away if that was what was meant to be. After all, you can't force a friendship. But I desperately did not want that to happen.

At precisely two o'clock, David Michael and I entered the Stoneybrook Elementary School playground. "I don't see why we have to come here to*day* when I'll be right back here to*mor*row. For *school*," whined my brother.

I patted him on the head. "You're going to have fun. We're going to meet Claudia and Mary Anne. They're sitting for Jenny and Jamie."

David Michael stopped in his tracks and looked at me with exasperation. "Jenny and Jamie? They're *three*," he said. "And one of them is a *girl*!"

"You'll manage. Anyway, I'll tell you a secret. I want a chance to talk to Mary Anne and Claudia. So you could help me. You could be, like, the junior baby-sitter," I said, remembering when I

183

had made Mallory a deputy sitter. "Since you're a first-grader now."

David Michael brightened. "Okay."

He ran ahead of me to the climbing bars, where Mary Anne and Jamie were sitting on the bottom rung, Mary Anne dipping her head to avoid the row of rungs above.

"Hi!" called David Michael. "Hey, Jamie, today I'm—"

"Hi-hi!" Jamie replied.

"Yeah. Hi-hi. Today I'm going to be the—"

"Hi-hi, Kristy!"

"Hi, Jamie."

"Jamie," my brother tried again, "today I'm going to be the junior baby-sitter. So you have to do everything I say."

"I'll explain later," I whispered to Mary Anne.

"Okay," said Jamie to David Michael.

My brother had been expecting an argument. He was surprised when he didn't get one. "Oh," he said. "Well, come over to the swings with me."

Jamie obediently followed David Michael to the swings, leaving Mary Anne and me behind. We wandered across the playground and sat down under a pine tree. We were very familiar with the pine tree. We had spent a lot of time sitting under it when we went to Stoneybrook Elementary ourselves, especially Mary Anne, who hated gym

184

and sports and organized games of any kind. She escaped all of them whenever possible and sat under the tree with a book or her troll dolls.

As if she could read my mind, Mary Anne said, "Remember when we used to sit here? You and Claudia and I?"

"I used to get away from Alan Gray here. He said this was a girlie tree."

I heard laughter and looked up to see Claudia and Jenny approaching.

"I remember that!" exclaimed Claud. "Alan wouldn't come within twenty feet of the tree if we were here. Girl cooties."

"Hey, Jenny!" David Michael flew across the playground, Jamie in tow. "I'm your sitter for the day. I mean," (he glanced at me) "your junior sitter. I'm in charge of you and Jamie. So come with me."

"Um, just a sec," said Claudia, eyeing Jenny. Jenny was wearing a dress. This one wasn't white, but it was very pale pink, which is as bad as white when you're at a playground. Her shoes were pink, too. Claud looked from Jenny to Mary Anne and me to David Michael. Finally, she said simply, "Try to keep her clean, okay?"

"Yup," replied David Michael, and he ran off with Jenny and Jamie.

"I told David Michael he could be a junior sitter this afternoon. He was mad because I made him come here to play with three-year-olds," I explained. "But this way, he's happy and we can hang out."

Claudia and Mary Anne smiled, and Claud plopped onto the ground. The three of us sat in a row, eyes trained on our sitting charges.

Mary Anne blew her bangs out of her eyes. "Hot," she said.

"Yeah." Claudia suddenly flung herself onto her back, then sat up again. "How did it get to be the last day of summer?" she cried. "It isn't fair."

"It did go by kind of fast," agreed Mary Anne.

"Really?" I said. "It didn't seem fast to me. You know what? I'm glad it's over."

"You're kidding, right?" said Claud.

I shook my head. "Nope."

"Then why? Why are you glad it's over?"

I shrugged. I found a twig and drew a sun and a smiley face in the earth.

"You're not going to tell me," said Claudia flatly.

I heard the hurt in her voice, so I dropped the twig and looked at her. "Yes, I am," I said. "I am going to tell you. I'm just thinking about how to explain things."

Claudia relaxed. "Okay."

Finally, I said, "All right. The truth is, I did something really stupid."

"You did?" Claudia raised her eyebrows. "What?"

"I convinced myself that my father was going to remember my birthday somehow. I even thought he might come back to Connecticut and surprise me. I don't know why I thought that."

I saw something slide into place in Claud's brain. *Click.* A connection had been made. "Because you wanted to believe it," she said quietly. "You needed to."

"Yeah."

Claudia swiveled her head toward Mary Anne. "Is that why you planned Kristy Day? Because you thought Kristy might be upset after her birthday?"

Mary Anne blushed and nodded.

"Oh, hey, but don't feel bad that I told Mary Anne about my dad and I didn't tell you," I said quickly to Claudia. "If it makes you feel better, she was the only one I told, and I didn't really want to tell *her*. She wormed it out of me." I gave Mary Anne a small smile. "I didn't even tell my mom. Anyway, it was a horrible summer. I spent most of it hoping for something that I was pretty sure wouldn't happen, and then it didn't happen, and I was still upset."

Claud inched over in the dirt and slipped her arm across my shoulders. "Well, if it makes *you* feel any better—you, too, Mary Anne—after all this time, Frankie dumped me."

"What?!" Mary Anne and I screeched together.

And Mary Anne added, "Of course, it doesn't make us feel better."

"Even though I was busy and missed Kristy's birthday and Kristy Day and a whole lot of other things? I hardly saw you guys at all."

"But we thought you were happy spending time with your boyfriend," I said.

Claudia reddened. "I'm not sure he was my boyfriend. At least, I'm not sure he considered me his girlfriend. I think I was someone convenient to spend the summer with because his friends were away. Only I didn't realize that until just recently."

"Oh, there must have been more to it than that," said Mary Anne. "I mean, I saw how he was looking at you at your birthday party."

Claudia smiled fondly. "Yeah. We did get off to a good start. We had fun for a while, but . . ." She trailed off and began picking apart a pinecone. "Um, guys, I have to ask you a question: What happened to us? I mean, to our friendship? *Ours*," she said, pointing to Mary Anne and me and then to herself.

"Excuse me, what?" I said.

"Oh, Kristy, you heard her," said Mary Anne.

"I know."

"We have to talk about it," said Claudia.

"Well, what happened to it is that all of a sudden you're interested in stuff like makeup and clothes and — and boys!" I exclaimed. "And Mary Anne and I . . ."

"Aren't," Mary Anne supplied.

Claudia smiled. "I wouldn't say it happened all of a sudden. But whatever. It doesn't mean we can't be friends. I *do* have to find out how to make room for *all* of my friends in my life, though. Being chosen by Frankie — because that's what it felt like, like he *selected* me from all the available girls in the world — was really exciting. A boy going into ninth grade singling out a girl who was going into seventh, and being impressed by her art, and wanting to go places and do things. It was like we were in our own world. That felt so special that it sort of expanded until there wasn't room for anyone else, even though I missed the things the three of us used to do together." Claudia exhaled loudly. "But then these last few days . . . after Frankie's final phone call . . . these last few days have been just awful. I don't think I've ever felt this bad, not in my whole life, and all I wanted to do was talk to you guys. But I was afraid to call you. I thought maybe you'd say 'I told you so.' Or even worse, that you wouldn't really care anymore. And I couldn't have blamed you. Then you called, Kristy, and the second I heard your voice I knew everything would be all right. I knew that even if the three of us are in different places at least we're still on the same side."

Mary Anne glanced at me. "I guess we did feel like you didn't want to be our friend anymore," she said to Claudia. "Or maybe like you didn't want *us* to be *your* friends, if you see the difference."

"Either way it isn't true!" cried Claud. "I've missed you so much!"

"You have?" I couldn't help saying.

And Mary Anne added, "We missed you, too!"

"What is true," continued Claudia, "is that we're not the same people we used to be. Mimi said kids grow up at different rates. But they all do grow up eventually."

"I think we'll have to try really hard," said Mary Anne thoughtfully, "to stay friends even if we keep changing."

"Do you think we can do that?" I asked.

"We'd better be able to," replied Mary Anne. "Anyway, here. I'll tell you a good thing that happened this summer: baby-sitting. Now I can baby-sit just like you guys. I don't even need a sitter of my own when I sit," she added, glancing at Claudia.

"That was a weird day," commented Claud.

"Maybe now my dad will get rid of some of his other rules," Mary Anne went on.

"'I believe in miracles!'" sang Claudia.

I heaved an enormous sigh and said, "Well, I'm glad we had this talk, but you know what? Everything still feels, I don't know, unfinished. Like, what *is* going to happen when we go back to school tomorrow? You have other friends now, Claud, and, I'm sorry, but I don't think Mary Anne and I are ever going to be fashion plates. My mom always talks about the glue that holds people together. You know, common interests or experiences or whatever. What kind of glue is going to hold the three of us together?" I paused. "And then there's Watson. What's going to happen with him and Mom? That's another unfinished thing. I know they're serious about each other. I wish I had a crystal ball. I'd like to look into it and see next month or next year. . . ."

"No, you wouldn't," said Mary Anne. "It's better not to know. Really."

"Aren't you curious?"

"Yes, but I'll find out anyway, without the crystal ball. Just more slowly."

"As for the glue," said Claudia, "I don't think we need to worry about that. There's more glue holding us together than . . . than . . ."

"Than one of David Michael's art projects!" I whispered loudly, picturing a macaroni structure he had made recently that had fairly dripped with Elmer's and had taken nearly a week to dry thoroughly.

Claudia and Mary Anne laughed.

"But seriously," said Claud, "think about it. I could feel the glue all summer, even when I was with Frankie, even when I felt so apart from you. The glue is here under our old girlie tree, and it's in every step along the sidewalks of Bradford Court, and it's in all the secrets we've kept—"

"Did anyone *ever* find out that we were the ones who made that dent in your garage door?" I asked Mary Anne, recalling the unfortunate incident, six years earlier, involving a bicycle that had had its training wheels removed a bit prematurely.

"No!" she shrieked. "Don't even mention it!"

"And," Claudia continued, "the glue is in the hours we spent playing Monopoly, and the school projects we worked on together. And it's in Charlie and Sam and David Michael, in Mimi and Janine and our parents. It's even in the people who aren't here—your mother, Mary Anne, and your father, Kristy."

"But most important," said Mary Anne, "it's in us. *We're* the glue. We're holding us together. Do you know what I mean?"

Claudia and I nodded.

At that moment, David Michael, Jamie, and

Jenny came running to us from the swings and halted, panting sweatily, by our tree.

Jenny's clothes were still pristine.

"I kept her clean!" David Michael announced triumphantly.

"Another miracle." I got to my feet. "Good job," I told my little brother.

Claudia and Mary Anne rose, too, brushing pine needles from their shorts, and we headed across the playground.

"I'll see you guys tomorrow," said Claud as she and Jenny turned toward the Prezziosos' street. "You want to walk to school together?"

"Yes! Definitely!" I exclaimed. "Claud, that will be great."

"Excellent." Claudia flashed a grin at Mary Anne and me, and I knew that the three of us felt as though a great weight, one that had been holding us down all summer, had been lifted away.

★　　★　　★

That night summer bedtimes came to an end in the Thomas household. (Well, Sam and Charlie were too old for bedtimes, but David Michael's and mine came to an end.)

"Eight o'clock! Are you kidding?" squawked David Michael as Mom led him firmly to his room that evening.

"This is your first-grade school-night bedtime," Mom informed him.

"Man," muttered my little brother.

By nine o'clock I was in my own room. It wasn't my new bedtime yet, but I was tired, and I didn't want to get off on the wrong foot in seventh grade. I turned out my lamp, knelt on the bed, and grabbed my flashlight. Mr. Spier's school rules for Mary Anne were back in place and it was too late for us to talk on the phone. But she was at her window with her own flashlight. We signaled SEE YOU TOMORROW and GOOD NIGHT and then I slid under the covers.

Two seconds later I was at my window again. I wanted to see one more shooting star, for good luck, before school began.

But the night was inky and the heavens were quiet.

Summer was over.

1 6   stacey

"I can't believe you're coming inside with me," I said.

I sat sulkily in our car, my arms crossed, gazing out the window at Stoneybrook Middle School and pointedly *not* looking at my mother.

Mom turned off the engine. "Stacey—"

"I'm not in kindergarten," I interrupted her. "I can walk into a new school by myself."

"We have already been through this," Mom replied patiently. "I need to talk to the principal and the nurse about your diabetes. Maybe to your teachers, too."

"*All* my teachers?" I cried. According to my schedule, I was going to have seven different ones, if you included the art teacher.

"Stacey—"

"Mom, it's my first day at my new school. Please don't ruin it for me."

"I'm not going to ruin it for you. But I do need to talk to the principal at least. And you're supposed to check in at the office anyway, so I might as well come with you. Honestly, I'm not going to embarrass you."

"Promise?"

"Promise."

"Okay. Just . . . please walk way ahead of me so no one knows I'm with you."

"How flattering," said my mother. But she was smiling.

Mom started across the lawn toward the front doors and I followed at a discreet distance. So far, so good. With any luck, no one would even notice my mother.

After a few wrong turns, Mom found the principal's office, and we spoke to Mr. Taylor—thankfully in his office with the door closed so no one could see us.

"Welcome, Stacey," said Mr. Taylor, and he shook my hand.

"Thanks," I replied.

Mr. Taylor sat down behind his desk, and Mom and I sat in chairs across from him.

"I see that you're an excellent student," Mr. Taylor commented, peering at my records.

"Thanks," I said again.

"Of course, it's just the diabetes that's a concern," said my mother. "Stacey was pretty sick last year."

"But I'm a lot better now. Everything is under control. I never cheat on my diet."

"Honey, the school needs to know what to do if there's a problem," said Mom.

Mr. Taylor glanced at the clock and then at me. "Stacey, the first bell is going to ring soon. Would you like to go to your class? I can talk to your mother alone. And introduce her to the nurse."

"Shouldn't Stacey be present for that?" asked my mother.

"I don't see any reason for her to miss out on the start of her first day here. A student guide is waiting in the vestibule. I can arrange for Stacey to talk to the nurse later."

I decided I loved Mr. Taylor.

Outside Mr. Taylor's office were two students who had volunteered to show newcomers around. When I approached them, a bouncy girl with a bright smile who was carrying a clipboard and wearing a backpack jumped to her feet and said, "Stacey McGill?"

I nodded, grateful that Mr. Taylor had closed his door before anyone could glimpse my mother inside.

"I'm Emily Bernstein. I'm going to be your guide today."

"Hi," I said.

"Did you just move here?"

"A few weeks ago. I don't know anyone yet."

"Well, you will soon," said Emily cheerfully.

She led me to my first class, pointing out the library and the cafeteria on the way. "Now, you'll have to find the rest of your morning classes on your own," Emily went on as we stood in the hallway, "but if you have any trouble, just ask for help. Everyone's really friendly here. I'll find you at lunchtime so you don't have to sit by yourself, okay?"

"Okay," I replied. "Thanks."

"Don't be nervous," Emily called over her shoulder as she hurried away.

And I wasn't nervous. I really wasn't. I was excited, but I wasn't nervous. No one knew me here. Not one single person knew that I had wet the bed at a sleepover or that an ambulance had had to take me away from school or remembered the zillion days I had been absent in order to go to some doctor appointment or other. And no one thought that I was someone to be shunned, teased, avoided, or gossiped about.

I let out a huge rush of breath and opened the door to my first class at Stoneybrook Middle School.

* * *

Emily was right. The kids at my new school were nice. Well, obviously, not every single one of them. I saw two boys slap another boy's notebook out of his hands, but eventually all three began to laugh and they walked off together. In gym class

I heard some snickering among the girls about an unpleasant odor coming from the coach's office. On the other hand, when I got seriously lost after my third class, I didn't even have to ask for help. A shy-looking girl with braids approached me and said, "Do you need help?"

"Is it that obvious?" I asked.

She smiled and shrugged. "Well, you're turning around in circles and looking at your schedule and all up and down the hall . . ."

"This is my first day here," I admitted. "I can't find room one-twenty-six."

"Oh. Just make a left up there and go to the end of the corridor. You can't miss one-twenty-six. It'll be on the right. Okay?"

"Okay. Thanks!"

I practically skipped around the corner. Things were off to an excellent start. My teachers seemed decent and reasonable (two of them were actually really funny), and none of them made me do anything horrifying such as stand in front of the class and introduce myself. If they had done that, I think I would have lied or at least left out a whole bunch of the sad parts: "Hi! I'm Stacey McPerky! I just moved here from New York!" (I would have omitted the word *City*.) "And, well, that's it! I'm just so happy to be here!"

By lunchtime I'd been assigned a little homework, but nothing unmanageable, and I still hadn't had any bad experiences. I was a teensy bit nervous about the cafeteria, though, and with good reason. As I stood in the doorway and looked around, my first thought was that the room was colossal. It was, like, three times the size of the cafeteria in my minuscule private school back in New York (City). I realized I didn't even know what to do. I saw several different food lines, I saw some kids paying with swipe cards and some with cash, and I saw soda and drink machines that seemed to be operated by tokens.

I was seriously contemplating just backing out the door and spending lunch in the library, knowing full well that skipping a meal would mess up my insulin, when I felt a hand on my elbow.

"Hi, Stacey!"

Emily was at my side. I nearly fainted with relief.

"Oh! Hi."

"You look a little confused."

"I'm a lot confused."

"Well, stop worrying. I'll show you what to do, and then you can sit with me and my friends."

I followed Emily across the cafeteria like a grateful puppy, and she helped me sign up for a swipe card, buy a pack of tokens, and then choose my lunch. It was an admittedly small meal, but by then I knew pretty much what I could eat and when. Emily eyed my tray, and I could see her thinking "Anorexia?" but she said nothing as we threaded our way among tables to a crowded one near the back wall.

At one end of the table were two empty seats. Emily slid into one before anyone else could claim it and indicated that I should sit in the other. When I did, every single person at the table turned and looked at me.

I froze.

Then I said, "Hi! My name is Stacey McGill. I come from another planet."

The kids laughed.

Emily said, "Stacey, this is Claudia Kishi, that's Dori Wallingford, that's Pete Black, and over there are Rick Chow and Howie Johnson."

Everyone waved or smiled.

"So?" Emily said to me as she picked up her sandwich. "How was your morning?"

"Fine. You were right. The kids here are nice."

We talked a bit, and I tried to match names with faces, but already I could remember only Emily and Claudia. Kids stood up and sat down. Other kids stopped by to chat. Everyone wanted to catch up on everyone else's summer.

Lunch period seemed to be over as soon as it had started.

By the time the last bell of the day rang, I was exhausted. I found my locker, successfully opened it, grabbed a few books, and made my way to the front entrance. I was crossing the lawn—and desperately hoping that I actually did know my way home, as I had assured my mother—when I heard footsteps behind me. Soon I was joined by Claudia Kishi, who was talking over her shoulder to two girls, one of whom had braids and I thought might have been the student who had helped me when I was lost.

"Bye, you guys!" Claudia called to them. "Are you sure you don't want to walk home with me?"

"We can't!" replied the girl with the braids. "We're going to go pick up David Michael at his school."

"Okay. See you later." Claudia turned to me. "I'm Claudia, in case you forgot."

"Nope. I remembered."

"And you're . . . Stacey?"

"Yup."

"Do you live around here?"

"We moved to Fawcett Avenue. . . . Um, I was just hoping that I actually know how to get back there."

Claudia grinned. "I live on Bradford Court. That's right nearby. I'll walk you home. So, Emily said you used to live in New York City?" I nodded. "How come you moved?"

"I—My dad switched jobs."

Claudia looked as if she were waiting for me to say something else. When I didn't, she said, "I love your earrings. They're really pretty."

"Thanks! And I love yours."

"Thanks. I made them myself."

"You're kidding!"

"Nope. I love art. Painting mostly, but I like to do other things, too."

I decided that Claudia also *looked* artsy. She was by far the most fashionable dresser I'd seen at school, with her big earrings and chunky bracelet, her bell-bottoms (which I was pretty sure she had decorated herself), and her fluorescent-green hat that looked like a bejeweled engineer's cap.

"Have you lived in Stoneybrook a long time?" I asked.

"My entire life."

"I guess that's as long as you could live here."

Claudia laughed. "You're so lucky to have lived in New York. I'm dying to go shopping there. All those clothing stores . . . Do you like art?"

"Well, not the way you do, I don't think. I can't draw or anything. But my mom says the way I put outfits together is artistic."

Claudia nodded. "You should come over sometime. It would be fun."

"Okay. I mean, thanks. I'd like that."

We managed to walk all the way to Fawcett without the conversation leading anywhere near diabetes or past bad experiences. As I walked through my front door, Claudia called to me, "See you in school tomorrow!"

"See you!"

When the door was closed behind me, I pumped my fist in the air and whispered, "Yes!"

1 7 KRISTY

I got the idea for the Baby-sitters Club on the first Tuesday of seventh grade. We'd been in school for a week by then, and things had gotten off to a very good start, despite what happened to me in Mr. Redmont's social studies class that afternoon.

It was a supremely hot day, so hot that the teachers in our unair-conditioned school had opened every single window and door, and Mr. Redmont had finally (when he'd noticed that nobody could concentrate on anything but the heat) let us stop working in order to make fans out of construction paper. The fans didn't do much except keep the bees away, but I took the opportunity, while I was cutting and folding, to think about Mary Anne and Claudia and me. Since our talk at the school playground, things had been better. We'd made more of an effort to see one another. We walked to school together in the mornings and occasionally walked home in the afternoons, and once Mary Anne and I had sat at Claud's table in the lunchroom. The table was crowded and noisy, though, which didn't appeal to Mary Anne, so mostly we sat at a smaller, quieter table. Claud had called me a couple of times for homework help, and Mary Anne had called Claud for fashion advice (even though she knew it would be hard to convince her father to allow her to follow the advice, which involved, among other things, wearing jeans to school). Still, sometimes I looked at Claud chattering away with boys or leaping on her bike for another shopping expedition downtown, and I felt that I was watching a stranger.

As far as my father was concerned, well, I just tried not to think about him too much. That was a lot easier now that school was in session and there were all the distractions of homework and trying out for teams and getting together with friends who had finally returned from summer trips and vacations. Had my dad even remembered I'd had another birthday? I didn't know, although I'd finally asked my mother about it. On the night of the first day of school, when I hadn't had enough homework to occupy my mind and it was past the time when Mary Anne was allowed to have phone calls, Mom had found me moping in my room.

"Kristy? Did something happen at school today?" She'd sat next to me on my bed.

I'd shaken my head. "I was just thinking about . . . well, about Dad, actually."

Mom had said nothing but had slipped her arm around me.

"Do you ever talk to him?" I'd asked.

"We're in touch, but I rarely speak with him."

"Do you think . . . do you think he knew it was my birthday?" I'd said, and then to my surprise I'd burst into tears.

"Oh, honey." Mom had gathered me up like she used to do when I was little and had fallen off my bicycle or lost a game of jacks to Mary Anne (which was humiliating since Mary Anne was so uncoordinated). "I don't know if he remembered, but if he forgot that doesn't mean—"

"Don't say it doesn't mean he doesn't love me," I'd interrupted angrily.

"But it really doesn't," Mom had told me. "He may have forgotten, but he'll always love you."

"He has a funny way of showing it," I'd said, sniffling.

"He has a funny way of showing a lot of things."

I'd pulled away from her. "Are you still mad at him, too?"

Mom had sighed. "I'm still disappointed in him, but I had to stop being mad. I stopped a long time ago because it was pointless and took up a lot of energy."

"Plus, now you have Watson."

"Well, now Watson has come into my life. But I don't know where that's going to go, Kristy."

Six days later, this conversation was replaying in my head during social studies, even though the fan-making had now ended and we were supposed to be engaged in a discussion about South America. When the final bell rang, I just couldn't help myself: I was hot, I was unable to concentrate, and I was so relieved school was over that I leaped out of my seat and shouted, "Hooray!"

Mr. Redmont looked shocked. He was probably thinking he'd been so nice letting us make fans and there I was, not appreciating it at all, just glad the day was over.

I sensed that I was in trouble.

Sure enough, Mr. Redmont said, "Class, you have your homework assignments. You may go. Kristy, I'd like to see you for a minute."

Darn.

But Mr. Redmont was very fair, and he was nice enough as teachers go, so all he did was ask me to write a one-hundred-word essay on the importance of decorum in the classroom.

"Yes, sir," I said, having absolutely no idea what *decorum* was.

★　★　★

That afternoon it was my turn to take care of David Michael. Mary Anne walked home with us, and then she and my brother and I sat at the kitchen table, drinking lemonade and waiting for the air-conditioning to kick in.

"Hey," I said to Mary Anne, "Mrs. Newton had asked me to baby-sit for Jamie this afternoon. Didn't she call you after she called me?"

"Nope. Maybe she called Claudia. I'm sitting for Claire and Margo tomorrow, though." Mary Anne looked supremely proud of herself.

Later the three of us walked to the brook with Louie and waded in the cool water. David Michael tried to make sailboats out of leaves and bark, and Louie ran around, looking for squirrels.

All in all, it was a pleasant, ordinary afternoon—not the kind that made me think anything unusual was about to happen.

★ ★ ★

David Michael, Mary Anne, Louie, and I walked lazily home. When we reached our driveway, Mary Anne whispered to me, "Nine o'clock, okay?"

I grinned. "Okay." Flashlight time.

When Mom came home a little while later, she had pizza with her. My brothers and I stood around the kitchen, breathing in the lovely smell of cheese and pepperoni.

But Sam and Charlie looked skeptical. "I wonder what she wants," murmured Sam.

I decided not to beat around the bush. "How come you brought home pizza, Mom?" I asked.

Charlie kicked my ankle, but I ignored him. "Come on. What do you have to ask us?"

Mom grinned. "Oh, all right. Well, you know I had arranged for Kathy Patrick to sit for David Michael twice a week this year to give you older kids a break, and Kathy called me at work this afternoon to say she won't be able to watch David Michael tomorrow. So . . . I was wondering what you guys are—"

"Football practice," said Charlie promptly.

"Math club," said Sam.

"Sitting at the Newtons'," I said.

"Drat," said Mom.

"But we are sorry," added Sam.

"I know you are."

My brothers and I dug into the pizza while Mom started making phone calls. She called Mary Anne before I remembered that Mary Anne was sitting for Claire and Margo.

She called Claudia. Claud had an art class.

She called two high school girls. They had cheerleading practice.

David Michael looked like he might cry.

Finally, Mom called Mrs. Newton and asked if she would mind if I brought David Michael with me when I sat for Jamie. Luckily, Mrs. Newton didn't mind.

I chewed away at a gloppy mouthful of pizza and thought it was too bad that Mom's slice had to get cold while she made all those phone calls, and that David Michael had to sit there and feel like he was causing a lot of trouble just because he was only six years old and couldn't take care of himself yet.

Then the idea for the Baby-sitters Club came to me and I almost choked.

I could barely wait until nine o'clock so I could signal the great idea to Mary Anne.

★   ★   ★

After dinner that night I went to my bedroom and shut my door. I sat at my desk and thought. I had three things to do: the composition on decorum (whatever that was), my homework, and some thinking about the Baby-sitters Club. I planned to do them in that order, grossest first.

After looking up *decorum* and discovering that I lacked it, I realized that, basically, I'd been rude. (Why hadn't Mr. Redmont just said so?) I wrote down some stuff about how being rude was distracting to other students and made Stoneybrook Middle School look bad to visitors. I wound up with a composition of exactly one hundred words (*The* and *End* being the ninety-ninth and one hundredth).

Then I polished off my homework, and finally I sat on my bed, smoothed out a piece of paper, and started making a list about the Baby-sitters Club:

1. *Members:*
Me
Mary Anne
Claudia
Who else?

2. *Advertising:*
Flyers
Telephone
Newspaper?

3. *Set up meeting times when clients can call to line up sitters.*
Where to meet?

4. *Weekly dues for expenses?*

My idea was that Mary Anne and Claudia and I would form a club to do baby-sitting. We would tell our clients that at certain times during the week we could all be reached at one number. We would hold our meetings during those times. That way, when someone needed a sitter, he or she could make one phone call and reach several different people. One of us would be available for sure. Our clients wouldn't have to go through what Mom had just gone through at dinner.

I knew Mary Anne would like my idea, and I was really hoping Claud would like it, too. If she joined the club, then Mary Anne and I would get to see her more often.

At nine o'clock on the dot I turned off the lamp by my desk and aimed my flashlight out the window that faced Mary Anne's room.

I flashed it once to let her know I was there.

She flashed back.

Then I flashed out this message (it took forever):

HAVE GREAT IDEA FOR BABY-SITTERS CLUB. MUST TALK. IMPORTANT. CAN'T WAIT. WE CAN GET LOTS OF JOBS.

There was a pause. Then Mary Anne flashed: WHAT? And I had to start all over again. I shortened the message. At last, Mary Anne flashed: TERRIFIC. SEE YOU TOMORROW. And we put the flashlights away.

I turned my light back on and was about to check over my homework, when Mom knocked at the door.

"Come in," I called.

Mom sat down at my desk and smiled at me. "I wanted to let you know that I'm going out with Watson on Saturday night."

I groaned.

"I'm not asking for your permission, Kristy. I just want you to be able to plan on my being out Saturday. Charlie's got a date, but Sam will be home."

I nodded.

"Can't you please give Watson a chance?" asked my mother.

"Maybe," I muttered.

I knew I was being a brat. So it was especially nice of Mom to kiss the top of my head as she was leaving the room.

"Going to bed soon?" she asked.

"Yeah."

Later, when I was tucked in, Louie snoozing at my side, I thought about the shooting stars and the summer, and all that had happened and all that was about to happen. What would seventh grade bring? Could I actually start a baby-sitting business? Would Mom and Watson continue to see each other? Would my dad remember my brothers and me at Christmas? (Here I sternly told myself not to start watching the mail until at least December 15th.)

I lay quietly, listening. Louie was snoring gently. Strains of music drifted in from down the hall. Through the open window I could hear a few frail crickets, the hoot of an owl, a car driving slowly along Bradford Court. Louie had flung one great paw across my back, and I slithered out from under it and knelt on my pillow so I could look outside again. Mary Anne's room was dark, but a light was on in her living room.

I tilted my head back, and to my surprise a streak of light crossed the sky—a flash as quick as the blink of an eye. One last shooting star. It marked, I decided, not an end, but the beginning of whatever was to come.